MAIN BITCH

THE AUTHOR

Bob George is the pseudonym of an ex-Metropolitan Police detective, currently working in security. Born in West Africa, where his father worked for the Colonial Office, George has been a judo instructor, and has trained as a boxer. He enjoys sports car racing, and driving his own cars.

MAIN BITCH

Bob George

First published in Great Britain in 1995 by
Allison & Busby
An imprint of Wilson & Day Ltd
179 King's Cross Road
London WC1X 9BZ

A catalogue record for this book is available from the
British Library

ISBN 0 74900 257 3

Typeset by N-J Design Associates
Printed and bound in Great Britain by
Redwood Books, Trowbridge, Wiltshire

To my father, for all his help

ONE

1976, early December. Britain lay beneath a hammer of bitter winds and heavy rain as winter came in with longer nights that magnified the unpleasantness. Big city thoroughfares lay deserted after office hours and, by midnight, the only people using the streets were those without a choice; people like Detective Constable Kinnaird who worked out of Fulham's CID office. He loathed the cold, a fact he was reminded of whenever winter came around. Every year he asked himself why he had never emigrated to the States and joined the Californian police instead of London's Metropolitan. The answer was always the same, at twenty the sun had not been included in his career profile. Ten years later he was paying the price. Alone he stared through the misty screen of an unmarked police car while an icy rain pounded a Fulham street, and the screen-blower struggled to maintain a clear view of a brothel opposite.

Kinnaird's partner and best friend, Greg Wright, was inside making enquiries about one of the girls who had been found in the street half-beaten to death. The police car had been warm and dry so they had flipped a coin to decide which one would make a dash to the brothel. Wright had lost, but that had been more than forty minutes ago and Kinnaird was beginning to wonder if he might have discovered other ways of keeping warm. He switched off the engine, turned up his coat collar and pushed open the door. The wind and rain rushed in without an invitation, soaking him before he was even out of the car.

The brothel was a three-storey building in Carnwath Road SW6 which had first seen the light of day in the thirties. Then it had been a medium sized guest house catering for a selective clientele. Things had changed. Kinnaird reached the front door and pressed a button beneath half-a-dozen other buttons with names alongside ranging from ELOquent Ella to ORIfice Olive. Subtlety wasn't included. The button Kinnaird used read Caretaker. Deep inside the building he heard a bell ring and waited patiently by an intercom while the rain soaked his coat and matted his dark, curly hair to his scalp. A minute later he was still waiting, wetter and out of patience. His finger stabbed the button again and this time remained there. The response was slow in coming, but a man's gruff bark finally crackled over the wire.

"Yeah, who is it?"

Kinnaird told him.

"Shit, not another one!"

The front door opened with a click and the detective slipped into a warm, inviting hall, the rain running off him quickly forming a pool at his feet. Red walls, carpet and lighting gave a hint of the kind of place he was in.

An old man bent with age, his hair whiter than snow, shuffled towards a small counter at the bottom of a staircase. Weighed down by an excess of woollen cardigans he leaned his elbows on the counter while staring at the detective. "What's the matter now?"

"Do you talk to all of your customers like that?"

"You ain't a customer!" He growled defiantly.

Kinnaird could easily have pulled him over the counter

with one hand, but it wouldn't have improved his disposition. The old man was Bert Ramsey, once Mr Big in the vice rackets of the forties and fifties. At his peak he had had a vice empire that stretched across most of South and West London. Then one day a competitor stuck a knife in his kidneys. He survived but his vice empire never did. Now burnt-out and bitter, he was caretaking for a successor he could only envy.

"Where's my partner?" asked Kinnaird.

Ramsey shrugged his skinny frame and brought three or four cardigans up around his ears. "If he ain't with you then I guess he's still up there." Kinnaird turned towards the stairs. "Hey wait, rooms one, three and six are occupied. People are sleepin'."

"Sure they are. Y'know one of these days the vice squad is going to close you down for ever."

"And one of these days the world is gonna end!" He shuffled away, angry at the world.

The detective climbed the stairs and moved along the landing, passed the first room and stopped outside the second. He rapped a knuckle on the door and pushed it open without waiting for an invitation. A chubby brunette with bright red, painted lips sat on the edge of a wide bed. A lot of effort had been used to squeeze her fleshy form into a black baby-doll outfit two sizes too small. Her plump arms wobbled with excitement as she patted the mattress next to her and flashed the kind of smile that invited abuse.

"Daddy!"

"Try again." Her smile quickly vanished as he showed his ID.

"Christ, not a bleedin' 'nother one!"

"I'm looking for my partner. He's a big bloke with reddish

3

brown hair and freckles. Have you seen him?"

"I've seen 'im." She swung a pair of thick, cellulite-packed legs up on to the bed then curled them under her heavy body.

"Mind telling me where he went?"

She shrugged.

"Let's make it easier, in which direction did he go?"

She nodded to the right. He thanked her and returned to the hall as a scream came from the room opposite. The door wasn't locked as he shoved a shoulder against it and burst inside. A naked couple sat astride a huge rocking horse, their backs to the door. The girl was in front bouncing up and down on the man's lap as she hung on to an imitation mane, oblivious to everything but her ride. Kinnaird took a step towards them.

"I never figured you for a peeper," Wright, his partner, whispered behind him.

"I was just making sure it wasn't you keeping her company."

The detectives backed out and closed the door without either rider being aware of their presence.

"I take it you came looking for me because you got worried about my welfare?"

"There are plenty of diseases a person can catch visiting a place like this. I'm certain a married man like you wouldn't want to make contact with anything contagious and, if I know Karen, she wouldn't be pleased with me if I allowed that to happen." Kinnaird leaned back against a wall. "So in all the time you've been here, have you managed to discover the identity of our attacker?"

"Would you be surprised if I said no? No one's that interested, even if it is one of their own who took a beating."

4

Wright sighed as if he were tired and opened a notebook, "All I've got is that our victim is a regular user of room five. Also, and this won't surprise you either, her real name isn't Sheenarena. It's Sarah Bankbird."

"I prefer Sheenarena."

"I found a couple of snapshots of her in the room along with some clothes." He handed Kinnaird the photographs. Both were taken with a polaroid. In one she wore a bikini, in the other nothing. "She looks better without all the bruising."

"And you got all this in forty minutes?"

"Like I said, no one's interested. We'll have to hope that she'll be able to give us some leads when she wakes up."

"As the others did, forget it!" Kinnaird shook his head. Sheenarena was the third prostitute to receive a beating within the past week. All three girls had been attacked at night and from behind. The only memory of the attacker had been a huge shadow with fists like steel.

"Why d'you think he doesn't touch their faces?"

"Who knows? He touches just about everything else."

The detectives moved slowly back to the stairs. Kinnaird was feeling sour, it was three weeks before Christmas and someone had forgotten that good will to all men extended to women.

"At least we know he has to be big."

"Yeah, but does that description fit any psychos you know?"

"A few hundred, but then most of them would've included pulping their faces. That bit has to be our clue . . . Maybe he's telling us that it's their bodies he's against?"

"Like some kind of religious nut trying to clean up the streets in time for Christmas?"

"Could be."

"I'd agree but for one thing, they all work for Duffy." Martin Duffy was the vice racket king of West London. Based in Fulham his criminal empire stretched from Hammersmith to Mayfair, covering the most lucrative market for sex in the city. At one time it was estimated that more than two hundred girls and boys worked for him. Duffy had risen to power swiftly, taking over the vice rackets of West London during the mid-sixties in a ruthless show of force that left more than a dozen dead by the time he had crowned himself. That was more than ten years ago, and though many had attempted to depose him, none had been successful.

"And that makes a difference?"

"Right now we've little else to go on, so I'm considering it. Someone might be settling an old score by hitting his women, or maybe it's the start of a gang war. Whichever, I'm certain the casualty count is set to rise."

"I prefer the nutter angle, it's so much simpler."

They reached the ground floor and turned towards the caretaker's back room. "So where d'you want to go from here?"

"Let's pay Sheenarena a visit at the hospital."

"I thought we'd decided that was pointless because she wouldn't say anything worth hearing?"

"In case we're wrong. Besides, at this time of night where else do we have to go?" Kinnaird knocked on the caretaker's door. It took Ramsey a few minutes to answer, and when he did he grumbled about never getting enough sleep.

"We're leaving," Kinnaird told him. "I thought you'd want to know."

"Why, so I can throw a party?"

"You're not very respectful to the law, old man."

Ramsey looked the detective up and down as if guessing

his weight, then spent a moment studying his face. Kinnaird was over six feet tall, broad, and the overcoat he wore added measurably to his sixteen stones. His hair was combed back at the front exposing a two-inch bottle scar just below the hairline, while a nose, broken at the bridge, completed the picture. He had dealt with most common crimes mentioned in the manual, plus a few that weren't. Ramsey read that much in his dark eyes before glancing up at his partner. Detective Constable Wright was about the same size and weight but where Kinnaird was swarthy, Wright possessed a ruddy complexion covered with freckles. His lazy eyelids meant he wore a permanently tired expression.

"There was a time when we might've banged heads," Ramsey declared, "but the past twenty years haven't been good to me and I can't do that anymore. So I use my mouth instead, because what you see on the outside ain't how it is inside. I don't scare easy, and believe me it's been tried by the best."

"I believe you, but someone used one of Duffy's girls as a punchbag tonight, then dumped her in the gutter like she was filth."

"I told your friend, I don't know nuthin', and that ain't changed since he asked."

"Was Sheenarena in here tonight?"

"Are you deaf? I said I don't know nuthin'!"

Kinnaird snatched Ramsey's cardigan lapels and brought him up close. "You want me to up end you and bang your head against the floor till you remember?"

"I told you that I don't frighten easy!"

"Yeah, you told me, so was she here tonight?"

The old man's long, lean hands squeezed ineffectually at Kinnaird's wrists while his face distorted with effort. During the seconds in which they looked into each other's eyes, Ramsey recognised something in the detective he had almost forgotten. It was the something he used to see in himself as a young man whenever he looked into a mirror. It lay just below the surface, an untamed turbulence that could wreak havoc, and the memory frightened him. Kinnaird knew he'd seen it and slowly released his lapels. Ramsey adjusted his cardigans so they sat properly on his shoulders then looked up, now subdued.

"She was here, but left on her own. I think she serviced about three blokes tonight."

"Not bad for a cold night. Do you know if any were big men?"

"How d'you mean big? I don't go up to their rooms for a peep," he sneered, his confidence fast on the return, but Kinnaird was waiting for a better reply. "I didn't see any big blokes."

"Any of the other girls entertain a big bloke tonight?"

"I ain't seen anyone big tonight, except you. I'd have remembered. Now is that it? Can I go back to bed?"

Outside the temperature hovered around freezing as the rain fell in heavy waves backed by a strong, unseen wind. The detectives groaned in unison as they climbed into the car. The seats felt cold through their coats, the windows were frosted on the inside, and the warm air had deserted the small cabin. The only redeeming feature was an engine that fired instantly into life. As they trundled away from the brothel, Wright played with the heater in an effort to coax some warmth from it and speculated on what they had learned.

"This bloke might be attacking them from behind because

they know him. Could be that he's a user?"

"Though the other two girls he hit can't remember having had any giants lately."

Wright gave up on the heater and used a hand to wipe the screen. "Maybe we're wrong about his size?"

"The girls were all picked off the ground, bounced against a wall and punched till he broke bones. I think big has plenty to do with his size."

"What about some kind of martial arts expert?"

"It crossed my mind, but I reckon someone like that would've thrown in a little style just to show off. You know what I mean, broken joints."

"Big it is then." Wright yawned and stared at the road ahead, the car's headlamps skimming over it. "I wish it wasn't so damn cold, but I guess that Italian blood of yours is suffering worse than mine, eh?"

"I think the Irish half of me is trying to balance things out, but it's hard when you're so cold even thoughts freeze in your head."

"Never mind, Del. It's only for a few months of the year."

"Yeah, but it's every damn year!"

When they reached the hospital the victim, Sarah Bankbird, alias Sheenarena, had just been sedated. A doctor told the detectives that after regaining consciousness she erupted into a violent fit, and needed to be held down until he managed to stick a needle in her arm. He further explained that she would have screamed the place down if her throat had not been swollen to twice its normal size. They were moving with the doctor through casualty towards another patient while Kinnaird asked questions.

"Did she manage to say anything which might help us?"

"She was in shock, it was all hysteria. Nothing that made much sense."

"Try me?"

The doctor stopped outside a curtained cubicle, "It won't mean anything." He sighed as Kinnaird folded his arms and waited to hear what he had heard. "Well, I think she said, `You . . . . you'. I might be wrong, but that's the best I can do, I couldn't understand anything else."

"When are we going to be able to talk to her?"

"She needs complete rest for at least twenty-four hours, perhaps after that. Now if you don't mind I've other patients." The doctor disappeared into a cubicle.

The detectives headed towards the main reception and located a uniformed officer who had been assigned sentry duty over Sheenarena. He looked and sounded bored.

"Is there any mileage in my hanging around here? I mean she's not gonna be awake until late tomorrow." The uniformed officer was called Ed Marsh, a twenty-year man and not a face Kinnaird knew that well, because it seldom got involved in crime work. Marsh was one of a breed, a uniform carrier, content to float along the job's surface and avoid involvement in anything until retirement freed him from the obligation. It was not an attitude Kinnaird cared for but then he had had it pointed out many times that he could be too dedicated. The uniformed officer stared at him with an intensity that urged release, but sometimes life could be tough, even on a uniform carrier.

"I need you here."

"Why?" Marsh didn't try to hide his disappointment.

"Because she needs twenty-four-hour protection, and for the moment you're it!"

The constable shuffled his feet like they were sore and

made clicking sounds with his tongue. That he was agitated was obvious, what wasn't was the reason why. It was night duty, it was freezing outside, the rain was falling. Finding somewhere dry and warm to stay had a lot going for it. "Exactly who am I supposed to be protecting her from?"

"The nut who put her here. D'you have a problem with that, Constable?" Kinnaird squared his shoulders as if ready to take on trouble. A detective constable had authority in serious criminal cases to give orders to uniformed officers, though the need rarely arose. It was one of those things not written down, but steeped in historical precedent.

"You can't really believe that he'd try reaching her in a hospital?"

"I think that's what I just said!"

Marsh dug his hands deep into his trouser pockets and hunched his shoulders. Kinnaird could read what he was thinking, something disrespectful about the CID, but the words never quite reached his mouth. "It's just that I hate hospitals."

"Beats freezing your balls off on a beat," Wright told him, as puzzled as Kinnaird by the constable's preference for the hostile weather.

"Only if you don't have somewhere warm to keep 'em, and I do." He winked as if letting them in on a secret.

"We need you here!" Kinnaird snarled, irritated that Marsh saw nothing wrong in finding somewhere snug and warm to be while his colleagues plodded the streets. He wasn't upset that the uniformed officer had somewhere to go but that doing so was irresponsible, and a twenty-year man should know better. If Marsh were urgently needed by another officer on an adjoining beat, then that officer would be disappointed, and it might just be a matter of life and death.

"Ok, ok but just remind them at the nick that I'll need relieving."

Sheenarena was wheeled out on a stretcher, and Marsh joined the orderly who pushed her in the direction of a ward. The detectives watched him without uttering another word before turning towards the exit.

The warmth in Fulham police station came as a welcome relief after the bitter cold plaguing the streets. The detectives wandered through an empty charge room into the front office in search of the station sergeant. Harry Phipps was a tall, gangly man with a dry wit and a heart of gold. He was in his early forties, and signs of ageing were evident by the streaks of grey in his otherwise jet-black hair.

"Have you two been drinking? Your noses are redder than a reindeer's."

They paused in front of Phipps' desk and stared down at him. "Del, d'you want me to carry the sergeant outside and drop him in the rain, or d'you wanna do it?"

"Whatever happened to your sense of humour?" Phipps grinned.

"It froze!"

"So why've you come to see Uncle Phipps? Think I can help thaw it out?"

"The tom who took a beating tonight needs twenty-four-hour protection." Kinnaird sat down on the edge of the sergeant's desk. "Until further notice."

"Mind telling me why, or is this going to be a twenty-questions exercise?"

"There's a chance that she knows the identity of her attacker, and we don't want her prevented from telling us. I told Marsh to stay with her at the hospital, he wasn't keen on the idea, but he's still there. He wanted us to remind you that he'll need relieving, and I noticed that he wasn't carrying a radio?"

"We're short on radios because they keep breaking down. Have you any idea the kind of hammering these blokes give them? Marsh volunteered to patrol without one."

"Making himself unreachable. Lucky for us he was at the station when the report came through." Kinnaird glanced at Wright. "Have any patrols turned anything up relating to the attack?"

"Not a thing. Everyone was indoors keeping out of the rain and not listening out for screams. Besides they hear quite a few of those in that area. No one notices anymore."

Wright pulled up a chair, "The trouble is sooner or later someone is going to die."

Phipps nodded, "What I don't understand is why he's hitting them on the streets and not indoors where he'd be warm and safely out of sight. On nights like this people tend to stand out and get noticed."

"So what went wrong?" Kinnaird shifted on the desk to get more comfortable. Wright yawned, "We were thinking that the attacks could be his way of cleaning up the streets before Christmas. Maybe all he wants is for the toms to stay indoors?"

"Correction, Greg thinks that. I'm still speculating."

Phipps grimaced, "Well, with this nut joining forces with the rain I imagine most toms taking the hint and staying indoors. It'll certainly be bad for business."

"That latest victim also works for Duffy," Kinnaird saw the information register in Phipps' eyes.

"Interesting, now I know why you're not so sure about it being a nutter."

"Well we aren't going to solve it tonight, so I reckon me and Del should retire to the CID office to contemplate and perhaps come up with a new direction to take."

"Contemplation," the sergeant frowned. "You mean the type that's done with your eyes closed?"

"Can you think of a better way to do it at four in the morning?"

Phipps looked thoughtful as he speculated on alternatives while the detectives headed towards an exit. "Y'know, sometimes you make me wish that I'd gone into the CID. It's got a lot of perks us poor relations in uniform never get to see."

"You can close your eyes in here, Harry."

"Yeah, but I can't lock that bloody front door and stop people seeing what I'm doing!"

"Good night, Harry."

Kinnaird went home a few hours later: to an Edwardian three-bedroomed semi in Bishops Avenue that faced the green fields of Fulham Palace park. His live-in girlfriend, Vienna, welcomed him with a pleased-to-see you sparkle in her eyes that meant more to him than anything else in his world. They had lived together since his wife had died more than a year ago. His marriage had lasted nine years, a disastrous mistake of youth that with the passing of time had lost the chemistry which had fuelled its initial passion. Yet it had continued to exist as a convenience. Separate careers had assisted in drowning their feelings for each other by dictating the different directions their lives took. He had grown aware of it, after a time, but perhaps waited too long before making an attempt to repair the damage. Mary, his wife, had grown determined to achieve success in her advertising career, making it plain that their marriage came second. She was comfortable with the way things were; they had a pleasant house, good cars and money in the bank,

14

plus she wasn't distracted by too many family responsiblities. His attempts to broach the subject of children were either ignored or avoided. She was too ambitious, too eager to reach the top, and once there, then, perhaps, they would think about a family. Vienna was different, not that she didn't want a career, something in the arts, yet there was an indefinable warmth about her, about the way she was. Sometimes he thought it was because she took an interest in him and what he did. Then, at other times, he would find them talking for hours on end, enjoyably so, about all sorts of things, trivia mostly, but she could hold his attention and turn the most frivolous topic into an absorbing issue. As for children, he sensed her career could always wait.

They had been thrown together during the turmoil of an undercover investigation, and experienced in days more perils than most people share in a lifetime. Vienna's mother had headed a protection gang Kinnaird was assigned to infiltrate. Towards the investigation's conclusion her mother had murdered Kinnaird's wife and attempted to frame the detective for the murder. Not surprisingly few had thought the detective's relationship with her daughter would last. Vienna was now eighteen, almost twelve years his junior, something which bothered him but not her. He knew that he should ignore what other people said about them, labelling him a cradle-snatcher. Even when it was meant as a joke he found it hard. Vienna understood, as usual, and guessed it was part of the reason he had never told her that he loved her, not in so many words. A bad marriage made him want to be certain they were a permanent item before committing himself, and that would take time. Besides, it changed nothing between them. In her eyes, Kinnaird's actions said it all. However, now and again she couldn't resist teasing him about it, and used her interest in astrology as the means to do so, because it exposed another supposed obstacle for them to surmount. As Pisces was her star sign she was not strictly compatible with a Gemini, his sign, and a bumpy relationship was forecasted. Yet the detective didn't worry too much about the stars painting a challenging picture. To him their relationship was lively because they bounced off one another in a way he had never experienced before and, for the first time, he knew what it meant to want another human being to know him as well as he knew himself.

Vienna had left for art college leaving him to sleep, and that was what he was doing when the bedside telephone rang. Semi-conscious, he commanded a bare arm to reach out from under the covers, yank the receiver off its cradle and haul it to his ear. "Yeah."

"Del, are you listening?" It was the kind of question people asked even when they knew the answer. Kinnaird gave Dick Clements, the CID clerk at Fulham, his best impersonation of a Chinese fast-food retailer.

"No Del 'ere. Dis take away restaurant. You want some flied lice?"

"You're in bed are you?" Clements ignored his weak ruse.

"That's where I go after working night duty, Dick, to bed!"

"Well, you'll have to get up. You're wanted at the Magistrates Court."

Clements' words took a moment to register. When they did, Kinnaird's eyes snapped open, "What?"

"Apparently you're witness to a uniform lad's arrest."

"Since when? I haven't gone witness to anything for a mag court in ages." Kinnaird brushed the sleep from his eyes and tried to recall his last case involving uniformed officers. All were pending an appearance at the Crown Court and, try as he might, he couldn't think of any due for a hearing before the local magistrates.

"Well, you did this time. It's your name the clerk of the court keeps calling out. You'd better get over to West London Mag pronto. I'll warn them that you're on your way."

"Who the hell's the officer?"

"New one to me, Del. Bloke called Bonner."

"What's the offence?" Clements hesitated raising Kinnaird's agitation. "I asked you what the offence was, Dick?"

"It's . . . . er . . . . an odd one for you to go witness on, Del."

"Just tell me what it is?"

"Drunk and disorderly."

He allowed a rush of anger to sweep through him before sucking in a couple of deep breaths and regaining control. "Tell me this is a joke, Dick. I'll laugh then go back to sleep. I promise no violence."

"Wish I could, Del. You'd better get to court." Clements sounded as if he were having trouble speaking, as if he were having to stifle something. Something like laughter. "Look on the bright side . . . . "

"There is one?"

"Always."

"I know this is a mistake, but what?"

"It ain't snowing," Clements guffawed down the line.

"You looked at the board yet, Dick," Kinnaird asked calmly, more calmly than he felt. The laughter stopped abruptly as the clerk examined a chessboard beside his desk, and spotted that his black king was in check.

"Damn it Del, you made your move last night. That's mate in two!"

"You aren't wrong, Dick." He cradled the receiver, climbed

17

out of bed, went across to a chessboard set up in a corner of the bedroom, and tipped the black king on to its side. Chess was a hobby he and Clements shared, and the two of them kept a game running at the office throughout the year.

It took Kinnaird a half-hour to get shaved, washed, dressed and down to West London Magistrates Court. PC Bonner greeted him as he stepped in through the main entrance. A twenty-year-old black man, fresh out of training school, the young officer wore a bright, genuine smile which seemed to miss the frown occupying space on the detective's brow.

"DC Kinnaird. Sorry to drag you in off nights, but this bloke refused to plead guilty."

The detective stared at him trying to recall when they had met, "What's this all about?"

Bonner's eyes widened anxiously, "Don't you remember, you said you'd make a note of it."

"Let me see your pocket book." The young officer handed it to him. The handwriting was neat and clear, an educated hand. "Now I remember you."

Bonner breathed a sigh of relief and looked as if he had just won the pools, "Great."

"Great nothing!" A little meanness entered Kinnaird's tone. "The next time you make an arrest with someone, find out if they want to go witness. Otherwise keep it to yourself!"

"But . . . but you helped me!" The young officer's words tumbled out. "I . . . . I couldn't have handled him without you." For a moment Kinnaird spotted something akin to awe in the young man's eyes.

It had happened one night when Kinnaird had been driving home just after a late shift. He had spotted Bonner having a stand-up fight with a man twice his size, and it looked as if the young PC were losing. The detective had pulled up, climbed out, and put Bonner's opponent on the ground with a few swift jabs to the head. To Kinnaird it had meant nothing. He had been a semi-professional boxer which made fighting drunks meaningless. To Bonner, though, it had meant a lot. Kinnaird found himself unable to hold his frown, and almost forgave him for disturbing his sleep. Almost.

"Learn a lesson this time around so you don't make the same mistake twice. All you've got to do is ask, it's as simple as that. You might be surprised to discover no one's that interested in going witness against a drunk. Especially if they're in the CID."

"Why? I mean you were there." Bonner looked as puzzled as anyone might who had just left training school and come face-to-face with the real world. Hendon spent sixteen weeks indoctrinating recruits with the law and police procedures so that by the end of training they knew how everything was meant to work. Sometimes, like now, it wasn't that simple.

"But you didn't have to say I was there, I wasn't wearing a uniform. I might've been a member of the public playing the role of a good citizen for all that drunk knew. My being here today is bloody inconvenient, or hadn't you noticed?"

"I'm sorry," Bonner resembled a man who had just been kicked in the groin, and Kinnaird suddenly wished he hadn't been the one doing the kicking.

"Yeah, me too."

"I'll go check how long it'll be before we're called." Bonner's bottom lip was trembling as he turned away and headed towards the courtroom. Kinnaird sighed unhappily and leaned against a wall while wondering if this was what it felt like to be a fallen hero.

"Who've you upset now, Del?"

19

The detective turned to see who was using his name and his face lost some of the seriousness. Brian Nesbitt was a detective sergeant at Fulham, and a drinking partner. "Hi Brian. Saw that, did you?"

"Was it really as bad as it looked?" Kinnaird explained what had happened and watched Nesbitt's eyes widen with understanding. "The kid likes to live dangerously, but how d'you think he took the tough talk?"

"Like he still has a lot to learn, and he will. Anyway, it's not entirely his fault, his skipper should've put him right about how it is with witnesses and drunks. I'll be pointing that out to Sergeant Crawford when I get back to the station."

"I bet." They moved to a position from which they could survey the entire crowd standing in the court's reception. It was a habit policemen grew into, but especially detectives, to keep up to date with which local villains were again before the magistrates. Men like Kinnaird knew most of them along with their families and associates. The majority of those on bail were in the gaol at the back of the court house, while families, friends and solicitors mingled together outside the courtroom waiting for their case to be heard.

"So what are you here for, Brian?"

"A couple of bikers who're going up the road. They GBH'd a bloke with a bottle, made a real nasty mess of his face. They're standing over there by the tempting piece in black, taking their time about giving themselves up to the gaoler."

Kinnaird spotted them. A couple of young, large, long-haired men, unshaven and wearing black leather jackets with Triumph motorcycle motifs on the back. In front of them stood an attractive fine-haired blonde packaged in a mini-dress, coat and matching set of thigh-high boots. She caught Kinnaird's eye and smiled. "Is she with them?"

20

"Believe it!" Nesbitt muttered. "She's the reason they rearranged the bloke's face. He took a fancy to her and tried his luck when he thought they weren't looking."

The blonde's smile grew the longer Kinnaird gazed at her. "Very nice."

"I'm trying to tell you it ain't very nice. She gets a kick out of men fighting over her. Also there's every chance her boyfriends won't go down. All initial witnesses have changed their minds about what they saw until I've only got the victim's word to take this case forward, and even he's starting to have doubts. They frighten people."

"It's OK, Brian, these days I only look at what's on offer in the shop window. Vienna's enough for me."

"I heard that, but her boyfriends haven't." Nesbitt nodded towards the two young bikers who were glaring in Kinnaird's direction. The larger of the two placed his big hands squarely on his hips and spread his shoulders. Kinnaird ignored him and returned his gaze to the blonde, whose eyes were beginning to say things with an X certificate.

"I think she likes me, Brian."

"Her friends don't!" Nesbitt sounded unhappy.

"I guess I really should stop staring at her." Kinnaird had no intention of doing that, not because he was interested in the blonde, but because the thought of the bikers getting away with a GBH piqued his code of justice, especially when the reason for it was a girl that probably met every man with take-me-to-bed eyes.

"You'd really make me a happy man if you'd stop blimping at her, Del."

"I know, but I don't want them to think they intimidated me."

"Does it really matter?"

"Pride, Brian. Pride."

"It'd be tough being proud without a face!"

"There aren't too many bottles handy for them here."

The blonde winked. Kinnaird winked back. Nesbitt groaned. The detective sergeant was forty with plenty of action experience. However, nowadays he preferred to avoid violence if at all possible.

"Are you trying to pull her?" He asked, irritably. "I thought you said Vienna was enough for you?"

"Just being friendly, Brian."

"By winking at her?"

"Isn't that friendly?"

"It's too bloody friendly!" The blonde's boyfriends shared a brief conversation without taking their eyes off the detective. Nesbitt suddenly glanced at Kinnaird with a little more understanding, "You want them to have a go."

"It's like this, Brian. If they think they can intimidate everyone including me, what chance does the world have. You might call what I'm doing a form of rehabilitation." He glanced at Nesbitt, "By the way, which of them does she go out with?"

"I never figured that out, they seem to be a team if you know what I mean."

"And I always thought three was a crowd."

Delaney removed his hands from his trouser pockets as the bikers began to move towards them, "Here we go."

The larger of the two stopped a couple of inches in front of Kinnaird while the other covered Delaney. "Wot the fuck d'you think you're gawpin' at, pig?"

Close up, the young man's long, brown hair looked in desperate need of a wash, something confirmed by a pungent body odour. Kinnaird didn't flinch. "At your blonde friend before you stepped in front of my face and fouled the air."

The biker's top lip curled back in an unsavoury snarl, "You think you're safe 'cos you're a pig and in 'ere, but you ain't!"

"Wrong. I know I'm safe because I'm me and you're nothing but slime!"

"You've just given yourself a heap of trouble, pig. When you're on the street you and I are gonna meet."

Kinnaird sniffed the air and creased his face, "Unfortunately you won't be able to sneak up from behind, so I guess I won't worry too much."

Someone screamed as a big right fist flew at the detective's head. Kinnaird ducked under it and slammed a right of his own into the biker's belly. The young man gasped and folded at the waist. The other biker stepped towards Kinnaird and Nesbitt stopped spectating by punching the young man's body twice in quick succession. The angle made the punches lack the strength to put him on the floor but were sufficient to catch his attention. He threw himself at the sergeant, grabbing for his throat. Kinnaird just had time to see it happen before the other biker regained his second wind and launched his own assault. The detective moved swiftly on the balls of his feet dodging a series of blows, then dropped the biker with a volley of head shots that spilled blood.

A crowd of uniformed officers rushed in as Nesbitt head butted his opponent with a crack that echoed throughout reception. A hushed crowd watched as the young men were quickly handcuffed and led off to the gaol. Oddly when people began speaking again it was in soft voices, as if they didn't want to be overheard.

Nesbitt's neck wore a series of deep red bruises that felt tender to touch. Kinnaird joined him wearing a bright smile, "Thanks for the help, Brian."

"I suppose you're a pal."

"We couldn't let them speak to the law like that."

"I don't think the law had anything to do with it, you were blimping their woman."

"Same thing, Brian."

Nesbitt looked doubtful, but just then the blonde wiggled across to join them. Close up she possessed no odour problems, while a pair of deep blue eyes were the kind to make a man think about innocence and beauty. Yet such thoughts died the instant she opened her mouth, "You made a right bleedin' mess of them!"

"You should keep them on a shorter leash," Kinnaird told her.

"I like a bloke who can 'andle 'imself," she smiled. "Gives me a warm feelin' inside, especially if 'e was fightin' over me."

Nesbitt moved away shaking his head like he had heard it all before, but Kinnaird wasn't finished, "I wish I could say it was."

"Y'mean it wasn't?" she asked, goggle-eyed with surprise. "But you were winking at me?"

"I had something in my eye."

"You wot?" Her loud exclamation caught the attention of the crowd, and some caught their breath as they waited to see the blonde throwing punches. "Are you sayin' that I don't know a come-on when I see one?"

"It happens." He moved away as Bonner called his name from a courtroom door.

The case against the drunk and disorderly took ten minutes to prove. The defendant was fined thirty pounds and given seven days to pay. Bonner apologised to Kinnaird several more times for disturbing his sleep before they left the courtroom. The young officer was so sincere Kinnaird felt a pang of guilt. When they parted at the court entrance he assured Bonner that he was forgiven, and that he would never mention it again. The young man appeared satisfied and moved away as Nesbitt joined them.

"I thought you'd like to know that you've a clear run at the blonde. The magistrates just banged up the bikers till their Crown Court appearance. So how'd you make out with her?"

"I didn't."

"It looked a dead cert, I thought you wouldn't be able to resist?"

"Thinking about my health was a major factor. I get nervous when a woman is that eager to get laid, also Vienna is the jealous kind, she wouldn't understand if I contracted something shared by the blonde's boyfriends."

"I heard you two were serious, but I didn't realise it was that serious. We've been friends a long time, Del, and I can recall you not being so choosy when you were married."

"There's married and there's being in love. Right now I'm enjoying the latter."

"Well I wish you'd thought about that before deciding to take her playmates on. I've more paperwork now than when I first came in here thanks to you!"

"No need to thank me, Brian," he grinned, and left Nesbitt on the courtroom steps.

At ten that same evening Kinnaird arrived at the CID office at Fulham police station. It was empty except for Greg Wright who was at his desk thumbing through the major crime book, checking to see if they had anyone to visit. He stifled a yawn as Kinnaird joined him.

"I didn't get much sleep. The council began resurfacing our road this morning, just as I nodded off. It's as if they were waiting for me to be on nights."

"Anything new in the book?" Kinnaird stifled a yawn of his own.

"A couple of daytime burglaries, a stabbing, a dishonest handling, all assigned. Nothing for us." Wright leaned away from the desk, "How come you look tired? Don't tell me they're resurfacing your road as well."

"I'll tell you about it in the car. What was the stabbing about?"

"Family dispute, a husband and wife. The husband caught a kitchen knife in the arm after an argument about the woman's mother. They'll probably be friends again by Christmas."

"Has anything new gone down on Sheenarena?"

"Nope, but would you believe that Parsons has been assigned the job? The DI obviously isn't interested in putting any effort into finding who's beating the shit out of toms."

"He can't appreciate what could be happening."

"He appreciates it, he just isn't interested. He wouldn't mind if every tom was found dead in the morning. He's got a thing about women, and toms more than most."

Kinnaird nodded and glanced at the crime book, "At least he's maintained the protection on Sheenarena at the hospital, though I doubt that'll last for long."

A telephone rang on Wright's desk and he picked it up. "CID."

"Another tom's been hit, Greg." It was Phipps, the station sergeant.

"How bad?"

"Couldn't be worse, her throat's been cut. It happened in

26

Seagrave Road, near the junction with Lillie, about twenty minutes ago. A woman heard her scream and called in. A couple of my blokes are on scene, the soco's been told."

"We're on our way." Wright gave Kinnaird the news. "Do you want me to call Colin Evans?"

"I'll do it." In the event of a murder, procedure required that the detective inspector (DI) responsible for the area be informed as soon as possible – in this case Colin Evans. Evans would then inform his direct line manager in the CID, a detective chief inspector (DCI) – George Ship, not because Ship would want to put in an appearance at the scene so late at night, it would be a courtesy call, a warning of what awaited him in the morning. At roughly the same time a similar call was being made by the night duty uniformed inspector to the home of the station's senior uniformed officer, a chief superintendent. When you had a murder, the brass wanted to know.

Evan's voice gave little away about how he felt, "I'll call the DCI from here, Del, and meet you at the scene in about twenty minutes."

When Kinnaird came off the phone, Wright asked how Evans had sounded. "Not good, but then calling him at home never does bring out the best in him." He paused briefly, "Y'know, it's odd, that tom having her throat cut."

"Maybe the giant got tired of using his fists?"

"He got his kicks using his fists, why suddenly switch to a blade?"

"He had to end up killing someone sooner or later."

"But not like this. It's a different MO." The *modus operandi* related to the practice a felon followed in committing an offence. It was a trademark, a stamp that made a crime specific to an individual.

"We'd better get going," Wright glanced at his watch. "I'd hate Evans to reach the scene ahead of us."

"So would he."

Seagrave Road junction with Lillie Road is at the northern most point of Fulham's ground, close to where F and B divisions meet at the border with Chelsea. If the murder had taken place a hundred yards further east it would have been a Chelsea problem, and one for the B division crime books. The murderer probably hadn't known that, and wouldn't have cared even if he had. Seagrave Road was a quiet, dark place in which he could kill and slip away unseen. Most of the houses near the junction with Lillie Road were officially unoccupied, condemned by the council for destruction, though often used by squatters, drug addicts and anyone else without a home.

The prostitute's body lay in a gutter beneath the glow of a curved Victorian lamp post. A couple of police cars had been parked either side of it while a photographer did his work. A small crowd congregated near the scene ignoring the cold, and chatting to the solitary policeman keeping them back. When the detectives arrived they pulled up alongside an ambulance. Kinnaird recognised a doctor standing with its crew and joined him. The doctor, Glen Morris, was in his late fifties and had a wealth of grey hair that never looked tidy.

"Been here long, Doc?" Kinnaird pulled the collar up on his overcoat as a chill wind blustered around them.

"Long enough for a brief reconnoitre only. Neat job by the way."

"And?"

"Quite a deep wound," he replied, very matter of fact, "but not hacked about, a very sharp instrument was used. There's some bruising around the exposed parts of the chest, and one hand looks like it's got a couple of broken fingers."

"What about her face?" Wright asked.

"Not touched, pretty though, or was."

"Is the bruising recent, I mean did she get it tonight?"

"At the moment all I can say is that she's got bruising." Morris was a very careful man who refused to be drawn no matter what the circumstances, and was respected because of it.

Kinnaird thanked him and the detectives walked over to the body as the photographer moved away. When they came level with her face Wright muttered an oath. Morris had called it a deep wound, but that had not prepared them for the red gash where her head had almost been severed.

Wright took a deep breath, "No one deserves to die like that."

"Except the person who did it to her," Kinnaird corrected, his expression growing dark.

A uniformed constable, the one who had discovered the body, joined them. He was a big man Kinnaird knew well nicknamed 'Pug', owing to a battered nose and ears acquired in a boxing ring. "Hi fellas."

"You found a winner tonight, Pug."

He glanced down at the body, his eyes watery, his voice a little choked, "Wish I could've caught the bastard. I really do."

"Are there any witnesses?"

"Nah, the old biddy who heard her scream didn't look out the window to see what was going on, said she was too scared. She simply called us. She's one of the few original residents the council haven't rehoused yet."

"Where does this old biddy live?"

"At number forty-two, but take my word for it, she's no help."

"You ever see this tom before?" Wright asked.

"Yeah," he paused and took a deep breath, when he spoke a tremor in his voice suggested that he was more upset than either detective had appreciated. "Her name's Tina Wilson. Twenty-one years old, a nice kid. She's been working around here for quite a while and never gave any lip. I guess she was on her way to a client at the West London hotel, that was one of her usual haunts."

"Was she one of Duffy's?"

"Nah, didn't like the big timers, though she does have a pimp. I only know his first name, it's Lenny."

"You ever meet him?"

"Nah, I visited her place a few times, but he was always out."

The detectives frowned at one another. Knowing a prostitute was one thing, visiting her at her home, another. Wright fired a question he and Kinnaird were both wondering, "Just how well did you know her, Pug?"

"I loved her." The big man stared down at the body as if unable to lift his gaze, his voice distant as he continued to speak. "She has a kid. Got into this game when her old man walked out on them. All she figured she had going for herself were her looks . . . . I figured different, even if people said I was stupid for doing so. But I guess none of us can help the way we feel." Kinnaird recognised the troubled look in his eyes and empathised. It was the same for him with Vienna whenever anyone decried their relationship, but Pug had carried even more problems. Tina Wilson was half his age, a prostitute, with a child by another man, hardly the credentials most men would care for. Perhaps Pug was stupid, but if Tina had felt the same way about him who could have said they wouldn't have managed? Kinnaird knew it was never that simple, that other people created difficulties, because what they thought and said had an effect, no matter how much you tried to ignore them.

"Who's to say what was right for the two of you? Not me." Kinnaird laid a hand on his shoulder. "I'm sorry she's dead, Pug."

"Did she live locally?" Wright asked

"Hurlingham Court." Pug was in his early forties, unmarried, with fewer than ten years to retirement. Perhaps he had been thinking about a new direction in life, something less solitary. A companion, particularly a pretty, young one, even a prostitute, could help make the future appear less barren.

"Pug, I want you to call Phipps, and ask him to send a WPC round to her address to check on the kid." The uniformed officer nodded, and Kinnaird registered the seriousness in Wright's eyes as he moved away towards a patrol car. "I don't think Pug's our killer."

"Me neither," Wright glanced down at the body. "But I'm wondering what Evans is going to think."

Kinnaird nodded. He knew that it had not been easy for the uniformed officer to mention that the dead prostitute had been more than an acquaintance, and not simply because it automatically included him on the suspect sheet. The job was full of moralists, and once word got out about them, Pug might find life a little less comfortable. For the moment Kinnaird would only allow word to get out if it were absolutely necessary. Wright agreed.

"At least we know it's probably the same killer."

Wright noticed an expression on his partner's face that he had met before. "You mean you've got doubts?"

"It doesn't make sense."

"So what're you thinking, that we've two nutters running around at the same time?" Kinnaird shrugged and Wright shook his head. "I reckon you just want to upset Colin Evans a little more."

"Is that possible?"

"Is what possible?" The DI asked as he joined them.

"That we've two attackers operating against the toms, and that this is nothing to do with a gang war." Wright glanced at Kinnaird as if expecting him to explain, but the detective suddenly appeared reluctant to expand.

"And what do you base that assumption on?"

"The way this one was killed," Kinnaird recovered from his silence and pointed at the gaping red gash, "is a different MO from the others. If she'd died from a beating I would have found it easier to believe the same person responsible."

The DI knelt down beside the body. The front of the girl's blouse flapped in the wind exposing her cleavage. He studied the ugly bruises across her chest and Kinnaird thought he heard him sigh before he rose to his feet. "You can still see she was a pretty kid, he didn't touch her face. That's the MO."

"I still don't think it's the same bloke." Kinnaird nodded to where Pug was standing by a patrol car, "One of the uniforms knew her. She lived at Hurlingham Court with a kid and pimp. I've asked for a plonk to visit the address."

"Duffy?"

"No. All I got was a first name. Lenny."

"She can't be much over twenty," Evans seemed to have trouble taking his eyes off the girl's face.

"Twenty-one," Kinnaird corrected.

"Same age as my eldest," the DI sounded distant, as if imagining another body in the gutter.

"Do you want us to start house to house, guv?" Wright

asked. "Most of them have got squatters in, but we might get lucky and find someone to come forward if we make the right approach?"

Evans dragged his gaze from the dead girl's face, his expression making him appear even more severe than usual, but neither detective could be certain he had heard what Wright had said. "If she doesn't belong to Duffy, then it seems less likely that this is gang-orientated, and points more to a nutter. No one can be unlucky enough to have two killers operating in the same area at the same time. I'm sorry Del but there's only one killer here, he just got tired of using his fists." Evans shivered as the wind suddenly whipped around them. "Del, I want you to pay her address a visit. Find out if she had trouble with anyone at home. Maybe she took clients there. Her pimp might be able to help."

"Do you want me to take Greg?"

"No, I need him here. We're going to work our way through every house in the street, and talk to every low life we can find. We'll meet you back at the station."

The doctor passed Kinnaird as the detective headed back towards the car. The medical man looked as grim-faced as Evans, and Kinnaird wondered about his own expression and what he must look like to the crowd. After ten years on the force people expected you to be accustomed to the horrors of a murder scene. That was what they said, those who didn't know better.

Tina Wilson had lived in a smart apartment building in one of the wealthier parts of Fulham. Hurlingham Court ran alongside the river facing towards Putney. It was the kind of place shared by rich retired people who preferred the big city to the countryside. Kinnaird guessed that the prostitute would not have done much in the way of home work, because that kind of thing tended to get noticed and would have been unacceptable. The detective sat in his car staring up at the apartment building while talking to Phipps on the radio. The WPC he had requested had been delayed by a drunk causing a nuisance along Fulham High Street. It meant that he would be going in cold in more ways than one. A pair of double front doors were governed by an electric lock operated by the residents. Kinnaird pushed a button for the porter. A few chilling minutes went by before a portly man wearing a brown uniform with gold piping running along its edges answered. Kinnaird showed the porter his ID but did not get invited inside. Not until he had explained why he was there, to see Mrs Wilson's child as there had been an accident.

"Is Mrs Wilson going to be all right?"

"Who else lives in her apartment?"

"Why er . . . . her sister and husband, and of course their little girl."

Pug had told Kinnaird that her husband had deserted her. He fixed his gaze on the porter, "Do you know if anyone's in now?"

"Why yes. I saw Mrs Wilson's sister arrive back sometime ago, and her husband is an invalid, he rarely ventures out."

"What's wrong with him?"

"Some kind of back trouble. It hurts him to do much walking."

A gap between the porter and door was enough for Kinnaird to squeeze in out of the cold. The porter looked a little uncertain as the detective asked for Tina Wilson's apartment number, but conceded when Kinnaird began to show signs of irritability. The detective made a point of thanking him and headed towards an elevator, changed his mind at the last minute and used the stairs.

He was keen on keeping fit, and was a regular visitor to his local gym, plus he would take any opportunity of making his body work, like sprinting up a staircase. When he arrived on the second floor his breath gave no indication that he had run all the way. A short hallway led to Tina Wilson's apartment, he knocked and waited. There was no reply and he knocked again, several times, until the door opened. A thin black man wearing a multi-coloured bathrobe stared out at him. He was in his early thirties with a mop of tightly knitted Rastafarian-style hair. He yawned, and didn't cover his mouth as he did so. Kinnaird caught a glimpse of half-a-dozen gold fillings.

"What can I do for you?" He had a West Indian accent.

Kinnaird showed him his ID. "Is this where Tina Wilson lives?"

The man rubbed his eyes as if clearing sleep away then produced another wide-mouthed yawn. "Yeah, but she ain't here right now. I'll get her to call you when she gets in." He moved to close the door but Kinnaird stopped it with his hand.

"She won't be getting in, that's why I'm here. Now I need to talk to you and I don't want to do that from the hall."

"What're you saying?"

"Depends on who you are?"

"I'm her husband. Now tell me what you've got to say, I don't like policemen in my home!"

"Tina's dead."

"Dead!" He repeated the word with what seemed like genuine surprise, except without compassion, love or feeling.

"Is your name Lenny Wilson?"

He hesitated, "It's er . . . . yeah."

"In that case I'm coming in." He pushed Wilson back from the door against a wall, then kicked the door shut behind him.

"Hey man, you can't do this!"

"I just did, Lenny, and by the way you're not her real husband. You're her pimp."

"I'm her common-law husband. I've all the same rights 'cos I live with her."

"You did, but she's gone, so you're short a meal ticket."

More concern registered on Wilson's face when Kinnaird drove that nail home than the mention of her death had caused. "How'd she die?"

"I was wondering when you were going to ask. Someone slit her throat."

He cringed and swallowed aloud, "Man, who'd wanna do a thing like that to Tina?"

"I was hoping you'd have some ideas, Lenny?" A sound behind them made Kinnaird swing round. A pretty brunette, around sixteen, wearing a short bathrobe, stepped out of a room further down the hall. "Who's she?"

"Get back to bed!" Wilson snapped. The girl took a long hard look at Kinnaird then returned to the bedroom. "That's her sister."

The detective left Wilson by the wall and ambled along the hall. Opposite where the sister had emerged he found the baby girl asleep in a cot, while a third bedroom appeared unused. A lounge had a large Christmas tree occupying part of a corner with a few presents already under it. He sauntered back to him with another question. "Where've you been sleeping, Lenny?"

"Hey man, that's none of your damn business!"

Kinnaird bounced him up against a wall and held him there by the lapels. Wilson annoyed him with the casual way he had acted after hearing about Tina's death. She had obviously meant little to him, and while she was out earning their keep, he was using her kid sister to keep warm. But more than that was knowing Pug, the uniformed officer who loved her, would have been the one to end up the real loser. People like the pimp had a bad habit of keeping contact with prostitutes they had operated. If Pug and Tina had gone together, he could imagine Wilson including himself in any of their future plans. Pug could have tried beating the pimp to a pulp to keep him away, but that would only have worked if Tina were able to put Wilson behind her, and Kinnaird had doubts about that, because toms seldom could. "If that kid's under age then I promise you're in for a very rough night."

"No man, no. She's sixteen, I swear." Kinnaird imagined Wilson to be a tough with the girls, but a sixteen stone detective was a different proposition. The pimp shrugged and faked a friendly smile. "Y'know how it is, man. Tina's out till all hours of the night, and her sister and me get lonely sitting around here."

"Is Wilson your real surname?" Kinnaird was suspicious. Pug had given him Tina's surname, but only a first name for her pimp. If their surnames were the same he figured Pug would have found that out.

He chewed on his lower lip as if he were having trouble remembering, but Kinnaird squeezed the lapels closer together and jarred his memory. "No, it's Jones. Tina wanted me to use her name when I moved in because of the neighbours."

"What about your back problem?" The West Indian passed

him a puzzled frown that answered the question without words. "She told the porter that you were an invalid, that you couldn't do much walking?"

"Oh that," he snarled. "She was full of excuses for the neighbours."

"She must have earned plenty to afford a place like this, must be fifty grand's worth. What I don't understand is why she allowed you to worm your way in?"

"She loved me, man, we goes back a long ways. Back before her other husband even."

"Is her sister on the game?"

"She's a good-looking kid, and she likes to wear pretty clothes. You work it out."

"Did Tina know that you were playing around with her little sister while she was working?"

"No reason she should, I didn't tell her and I know Bianca didn't." Jones suddenly saw the direction in which the questions were headed, and quickly added, "Man, my sleeping with her sister wasn't a reason I'd kill her."

"She might've chucked you out if she'd known. The way I see it, you had a lot to lose."

"She was worth more to me alive than dead, man. Even a cop must be able to understand that!"

"Have you been out tonight?"

"No way. I haven't been outside for a couple of days. Bianca will tell you, she came back early and I was here."

"Did Tina keep a diary or a list of clients?"

Jones frowned as if his memory were having trouble again. Kinnaird applied a little more pressure to the lapels. "Yeah, it's in the bedroom."

They walked passed her sister's bedroom to the one Jones and Tina had used. It was neat, clean and tastefully decorated in shades of pink and white. The diary sat on a bedside table. The detective picked it up and flicked through its pages. There were no names, but plenty of initials alongside telephone numbers, no addresses. Kinnaird slipped the diary into a pocket and returned his attention to Jones.

"I want you to think even harder than you did to find this, because I want her killer. Has she complained about anyone being rough with her lately?"

"A couple," he replied in a whisper.

"Regulars? Did they ever come here?"

"Yeah," he sighed and sat down on the bed. Suddenly he seemed to be carrying a lot of problems and it was obvious he had doubts about discussing them, especially with a detective.

"Have you ever seen them?"

"I seen one."

"How come a clever bloke like you only ever saw one? Remember, I know about your back problem."

"Tina didn't like me being here when they visited her, they were special. It wasn't just anyone she would allow to come to this place. She was worried about the neighbours and her reputation."

"Did Tina ever work for Duffy?"

"No, but she used one of his hotels and paid him a small percentage for the privilege."

"A small percentage? That doesn't sound like Duffy. How come he was being generous?"

"I did him a favour one time."

It was difficult for Kinnaird to imagine what Jones might have done for a big-time operator like Duffy. "So tell me about this person you saw pay Tina a visit here?"

"A big bloke, bigger even than you. About six seven. She

said he liked to slap her around while they were doing it, only lately she'd been taking a heavy pasting. He made her black and blue the last time he came. His name was Hastings, that's all I know."

"What about the one you didn't see? What can you tell me about him?"

"Only that he was a she. She was meant to be quite a looker too, so Tina said. Trouble was she liked to claw people, enjoyed seeing 'em bleed. One time she did it so bad I almost took Tina to hospital."

"What stopped you?"

"Tina did. It had been an expensive month, and we owed a lot of bills. She wouldn't quit working until she had enough dosh to cover everythin'."

"And you helped by staying indoors and servicing her sister."

"That's our business, man."

"Yeah, sure it is. Can you describe the woman to me? Was she big, small or what?"

"Tall, taller than Tina anyhow, and with red hair."

"What else?"

He made a face which suggested there was nothing else, then added, "She never let herself be touched. It was all one way. I think she got off on Tina being at the receiving end of things. She used to tie Tina's hands behind her back. She paid good, so we let it happen."

"How old is she?"

"I dunno, but Tina did say she was very strong, and Tina weren't no wimp."

"When was the last time Tina had either of them visit?"

"A few weeks ago, not long. They were both pretty regular."

A knock at the front door announced the arrival of the WPC from the station. Kinnaird stood beside Jones when he opened the door.

"We were asked to come over, something about a child?" Pamela Groove, the WPC, smiled when she spotted Kinnaird, while a seventeen-year-old cadet beside her stared uncertainly at Lenny Jones.

"And I thought it was because you wanted to see me," the detective joked.

"They didn't say how big a child!" She led the cadet inside.

"This ain't good man. That uniform will make people think we're criminals." Jones sounded deeply concerned. "Tina wouldn't like it."

"You are a criminal, but I told the caretaker there'd been an accident. He'll see to it that none of the neighbours think we're here to arrest anyone. Not yet, anyway."

"Someone from the social services is on the way, Del." The WPC glanced at Jones, who was looking more anxious by the second. "They have to check that the child is all right. You'd better get dressed before they get here."

"I don't like this. I've been helpful man, and the kid will be OK. It's almost Christmas, can't you just leave us alone? I'll look after her."

"The same way you've looked after Tina's sister?"

"Man, that's unfair." His head shook slowly as if he didn't deserve criticism. Perhaps he was being genuine about taking care of the child, but his track record to date was too poor to be ignored. "There's a big difference between the two."

"You're lucky, Lenny, it's not me that you're going to have to convince . . . . But what would be a good start is if you found yourself a job!"

"A job?"

41

Mention of work was something Jones obviously found hard to digest. "You should try it, it could be the making of you."

"What's happening, Lenny?" Tina's sister emerged from the bedroom dressed in a T shirt and jeans, her pretty face anxious. The hall suddenly seemed crowded, but this time the young girl wasn't about to let herself be fobbed off. "You want us to tell her?" Kinnaird asked as the WPC stepped forward.

"Tell me what, Lenny? What's happened?"

"How old are you?"

She frowned, her dark eyes growing angry, "Almost seventeen. What's that got to do with anything?"

"What time did you get home this evening?"

"About six, why?"

"And what time did Lenny get in?"

"He wasn't out."

"When did he go out?"

Jones swallowed aloud but kept his eyes on Kinnaird as they waited to hear the young girl's reply. "He hasn't been out, he's been with me all evening. Now, what is this?"

"Maybe he slipped out while you were asleep?"

"I haven't been asleep!"

"Looks like you've got an alibi, Lenny." He saw the relief wash over the other man's eyes. "Do you usually look after Tina's baby while she's away?"

"Yes, what of it?"

The West Indian turned to the girl, "I'll explain things to her, give me a few minutes." He led her back into the bedroom and closed the door.

"The baby's sleeping in there," Kinnaird nodded towards the other bedroom. "The bloke who's talking to the dead

42

girl's sister is a pimp, and also the common-law husband of our dead victim."

"Do you have anything else to do here, Del?" The WPC asked.

"Not for now. It's all yours."

"Thanks. By the way, when are we going for another drink? I'd like to see Vienna again, and so would Bill. It's Christmas in a few weeks and we were hoping for a little get-together before then?"

"I'll ask Vie, she makes all the arrangements. By the way, I hope you've bought me a big present."

"Likewise," she laughed as Kinnaird waved and disappeared through the front door.

Two

Wright and Evans were drinking hot black coffee while discussing the murdered prostitute when Kinnaird returned to the CID office. Evans looked tired, sleep dragging heavily on his eyelids.

"How'd you make out at the girl's pad?" The detective handed the DI the diary he had taken from the apartment, and watched while Evans scanned through several pages. "Busy girl, wasn't she?"

"The pimp she kept in the lap of luxury made certain of that. At least he was able to tell me about a couple of problem clients she had. One was a big bloke called Hastings who got his rocks off slapping her around."

"How big?" Wright interrupted.

"Around six seven. Could be our guy. Apparently he left her with some war wounds after his last visit, and was growing noticeably rougher." The other detectives looked at each other as if they had just won a prize. "There's more, a second client. A woman, redhead, good-looking, tall and very strong. She enjoyed making Tina bleed. Our victim was a hospital case after this client's last visit. I didn't get a name, but apparently she had another quirk, she didn't like to be touched. She simply wanted to do things to Tina."

"Jesus," Evans shook his head disgustedly. "I never cease to be amazed by the oddballs walking around this planet.

Let's hope the diary comes up with a name for her too. What about the kid?"

"Tina's sister lives at the apartment and gave her age as sixteen. I discovered that the pimp's balling her, so there's a chance she lied about her age. Apparently Tina didn't know they were at it. As it is, the sister takes care of the baby when she's not working the streets. It's an expensive pad, and up until now I'd say the kid's been pretty well looked after, but things could change. I left a plonk and cadet waiting for the social services people to show. It's their problem."

"What about the pimp? Could he be our man? Sounds as if he had a motive."

Kinnaird poured himself a black coffee from a jug Wright had brought in, "His name's Lenny Jones, a West Indian. He isn't the killer, too small."

"Pity." Evans finished his drink.

"What about Sheenarena?" Kinnaird pulled up a chair and sat down. "Greg couldn't find anything new in the crime book?"

"Parsons is on that one isn't he?" The DI asked the question wearing a puzzled frown, even though they knew he was aware of the answer. It had been his decision to assign Parsons.

"That's right." Wright sounded disgusted which didn't go unnoticed by either of them.

"I don't like wasting good manpower on rubbish!" Evans replied, annoyed by Wright's response, but he relented almost immediately. "However, once people start dying I guess I don't have a choice. Do you two fancy taking on the tom assaults?"

"Don't the assaults and murder go together, I mean how can we concentrate on one without the other?" Kinnaird studied the DI with curiousity, sensing something unusual was about to be put to them.

"A squad will be formed to deal with the murder, and no they don't necessarily go together. You were the one who pointed out that this was a different MO from the beatings. I want to keep them separate for the time being, but maybe you can bring them together, see what you can dig up. Concentrate on the backgrounds of each girl."

"What about Hastings and the redhead?"

"They're in with the murder investigation, forget them for now."

Kinnaird sighed and rubbed the back of his neck. "Working nights won't make following up enquiries easy."

"I'm sure you'll still find out more than Parsons."

"That really isn't a compliment, Colin," Wright told him.

Evans grinned, and some of his tiredness faded. "Parsons told me Sheenarena refused to talk, and not only because she's got a sore throat. She sounds really scared."

"Anyone who took a beating like she did is bound to be scared, or maybe Parsons isn't bright enough even to figure that out." Wright didn't try hiding his contempt, but the DI gave him a withering look that suggested he should.

"Well, I'd like to know if there's more to it than that. By rights she should be more than willing to help us find this creep. She still has the guard, but if she doesn't come across with anything real soon, I'll have him withdrawn. Maybe then we'll see how scared she can really be."

"Do you have any objections to us telling her what happened to Tina?"

"Anything's worth a try." Evans looked at his watch and yawned. "I'll leave you to it. I'm going home for a few hours' sleep, I've a feeling tomorrow's going to be a busy day. Just don't cause a riot down at the hospital. They may not be too impressed by your idea of visiting hours, and I don't want to be disturbed for a second time tonight."

Evans had been right about the hospital staff, none the detectives met thought it a good idea for them to question a patient at two in the morning. As they strode towards Sheenarena's room, a small Irish sister argued with Kinnaird after sending a nurse in search of a doctor.

"Sister, we're trying to prevent this from happening again, and the only way we're going to be able to do that is by talking to this girl, or don't you think one corpse is enough for tonight?"

"I must still insist that you wait until a doctor arrives before you disturb her!"

Sheenarena's room was twenty feet ahead when Wright said, "Where's the PC meant to be guarding her?"

"Off to the loo I shouldn't wonder." The sister was distracted long enough for Kinnaird to step around her and reach for the door. She grabbed his arm, but he was all ready pushing it open, "You musn't go in there!"

The sister got between him and the door, making him too busy with her to avoid a chair that swung through the air and bounced off the side of his head. He dropped like a stone taking the sister down, pinning her beneath him, his face pressed to the floor. Semi-conscious, his focus was a mish-mash of colour and blurred images, while sounds merged into a sudden burst of shouted excitement. Then someone crashed down beside him, and the only sounds came from the sister as she frantically struggled to get free from his bulk. Kinnaird tried blinking to uncloud his multi-coloured vision, and was briefly successful. A pair of gold, strapless high heels stepped in front of him. A woman! He felt elated that something had registered. A moment later his hearing returned. Someone was screaming so loud it filled his head. He squeezed his eyes tightly shut, an automatic reaction to the throbbing in his skull. The screaming ended abruptly, turning into a gurgling splutter before total silence. He realised with surprise that his eyes refused to reopen, and quickly the cold blackness of unconsciousness swept up and took him.

When the veil of darkness lifted a few minutes later his face was still pressed against the floor, but now there was something new, something wet and red that blended with the floor tiles as it lapped at his face. He could feel the sister beneath him, cushioning his body. She was still, perhaps waiting for help. He concentrated his energy into his arms to push himself up so that she might get free. It was a titanic struggle, but slowly his top half lifted clear as the pain flooded back, a distant echo which grew rapidly until it surged up his gullet and almost made him spew.

A frantic tapping from behind made him look round. A nurse stopped running and stared down at him. Her face a pasty white, her hands covering her mouth, her only comment, "Oh my God!"

More hurried tapping echoed along the corridor as other people joined her and stared down at the detective. He momentarily wondered if they were impressed by the way he could keep his head off the floor, then his arms lost what strength they had and his head met the tiles with a thud. He drifted somewhere on the edge of consciousness, aware of being lifted from the sister and gently laid out on a stretcher. When he opened his eyes a face was close.

"You're going to be all right," it told him.

He tried to reply, but his mouth ignored his brain. His eyes closed and the cold blackness took him completely.

Daylight streamed in through the large windows of a hospital room as Kinnaird returned from unconsciousness. His head ached, a throbbing, distant drum that touched the nerves at the side of his brow, a reminder of what had happened. Gingerly, his fingertips examined his skull running over a heavy bandage that covered his head.

"You took your time joining me."

Wright smiled at him from the only other bed in the room. His partner lay stretched out on his stomach with a drip feeding his arm. Kinnaird turned to face him and the room suddenly revolved, while an all too familiar nausea caught in his gullet. He waited until things settled down again before attempting to speak, when he did it came out in a whisper, "What happened?"

"Sheenarena's dead." Wright grew serious. "The PC guarding her died as well. After the killer decked you with a chair we had a tussle, but he wasn't alone. His friend jammed a blade in my back."

"What about the sister?"

"Another victim. She was screaming her head off trying to get out from under you. They cut her throat, same as Tina Wilson. When they finally picked you off the floor you were soaked in her blood."

"Did you get a look at either of them?"

"The one who hit you wore a balaclava, and I didn't get a chance to see the other."

"How come they left us alive?"

"The sister's screaming must've spooked them."

"What a mess." Kinnaird resisted the urge to shake his

head and stared up at the ceiling instead.

"That's the way Evans sees it. He's been in three times since last night. After each time I feel worse and wish we'd done better."

"Who was the PC that got killed?"

"A sprog. Young bloke named Bonner. I didn't know him."

"Shit," Kinnaird groaned aloud, an image of the young policeman appearing in front of him. "How long am I expected to stay here?"

"Another twenty-four hours I reckon, but you're lucky. With me they're talking New Year!"

"I don't feel lucky," Kinnaird threw the covers aside and swung his legs over the floor. At about the same time the door opened and Colin Evans joined them, following behind a small Asian doctor.

"Ah, good, you're awake." The doctor sounded more surprised than Kinnaird considered necessary.

"Either that or this is a bad dream."

"A nightmare," the DI corrected.

The doctor stopped beside Kinnaird's bed and gently pushed the detective on to his back. "Your inspector, among others, including a very pretty young woman, all want to talk to you, but first you need an examination."

"I feel fine, doc. Is Vienna here?" He looked at Evans, but the doctor hadn't finished.

"I think I should be the judge of whether you're fine or not. Now lie still and let me decide." The examination lasted five minutes, after which Kinnaird felt ready to throw up. The doctor smiled at him as if he had no idea, but the detective had doubts. "There, now you are ready to talk." He turned to the DI, "But no more than ten minutes, please, and the same for your young lady."

Evans nodded and waited until the doctor had left them, "What the hell happened, Del?"

"I thought we already discussed that," Wright interrupted. "We got caned!"

"That wasn't good enough the first time I heard it."

"It happened too quickly, Colin, they surprised us." Kinnaird recalled Bonner, the young, fresh faced uniformed officer, and guessed that it had been the same for him.

"Not half as much as they surprised me when I received a call at home telling me about it!" Evans had a way of making people feel that they should have done better, no matter what the circumstances. "They killed one of our blokes and a sister for God's sake!"

"At least we know there's two of them," Wright shifted uncomfortably, irritated by Evans' continued criticism.

"Yeah, we know there's two, but that ain't worth a fig without a description. You're meant to be detectives, that should mean you spot things. Descriptions are part and parcel of you being good at your job, that's what you've been trained for. But all that training appears to have been wasted. Especially yours, Greg. All you've proved is that you can count to two!"

"One of them's a woman," Kinnaird said, a vague memory of gold, strapless high heels returning to his aching head. Evans fell silent, full of anticipation as he sat on the edge of the detective's bed. "I saw her legs while I was laid out on the floor."

"Can you tell us anything else about her?" The DI leaned towards him, grimly intense.

"I think she's white, but my memory's hazy. I only got a snapshot of her legs just before I passed out."

"Didn't Lenny Jones mention a woman who almost

hospitalised Tina Wilson?"

Kinnaird nodded, and the pain in his head responded sharply, making him wince. "A redhead."

"Maybe," Wright added. "But she wouldn't let Tina touch her." The others waited for him to explain further.

"I think it's odd that someone involved in a sex romp won't allow themselves to be touched. She might've had something to hide? Maybe she was wearing a disguise?"

"I didn't ask Lenny her colour," Kinnaird said. "You might trace her from the diary, guv."

"It's still being checked." Evans turned away. "By the way we only found one set of initials which might've tied in with that hitter called Hastings, except the phone number turned out to be a call box."

"What's your next move?"

"I've more than fifty officers working on this investigation, but it's slow, and now that you two are out of it I don't imagine things will get any easier."

"I'll be back with you tomorrow." Kinnaird told him.

"Only if the doc says so. That skull of yours took quite a wallop, and it sounds like they'll want to keep you for a few days yet. Damn inconvenient I told them!"

"I can sign myself out."

The DI leaned forward on the bed, "But you wouldn't be able to return to duty, not until you're properly rested. Sending you out on the streets like this would be more than my job's worth." Evans rose from the bed and stretched himself before turning towards the door. "I'll send Vienna in."

When they were alone Wright sighed, "I swear that bloke gets grouchier by the day."

"He hates being proved wrong, and this thing's getting bigger than he thought." Kinnaird's girlfriend stepped through the door and the detective fell silent as their eyes embraced while she moved to his side. Her complexion seemed paler than usual, and he could see that she had been crying. He took her hand and smiled, "I'm all right."

"I was frightened."

He sat up and pulled her close, ignoring the ache in his head. She felt soft, warm, and unusually tense. Her hand gently caressed his cheek before she kissed him. "You know that I'll always be all right, you've told me so a hundred times because you've checked out my horoscope."

"Funny how I didn't even think about that when they told me you'd been hurt." She sat on the edge of the bed holding his hand tightly as if worried she might lose him. "I was being silly . . . . You'd think after what we've been through that I'd know you're indestructible."

"No one ever worried about me like this before, except perhaps my folks. It's kind of nice."

"Have you any idea what's going on or who's behind it?"

"I think it's something to do with Duffy." He saw the vice king's name register in Vienna's hazel eyes. At one time or other, through her family's connections, she had met, and was on speaking terms with, most of the major criminals in West London.

"Would you like me to do anything?"

"No," he shook his head, and abruptly wished he hadn't, a shooting pain made his eyes water. She gripped his hand tighter than before until the pain eased.

"Why won't you let me see what I can find out? I might be able to save a lot of time."

"This is too rough, and I don't want you taking any chances. I'll be out of here soon, and I'll find them." Whenever a difficult investigation came up it was always the same, Vienna

53

wanted to help. Since moving in with Kinnaird she had distanced herself from the underworld contacts she had known through her family. He preferred it that way, saw no reason for her to do otherwise. But that didn't stop her wanting to help, no matter what the risks. "Promise me that you won't do anything?"

"I think you're being unfair. You put your life on the line and expect me to sit back and take it, that's not my style."

"When I'm in a hospital bed, that's as fair as I get where you're concerned!"

She hesitated, a flash of anger lighting up her eyes, but it quickly vanished, replaced by a smile and something more understanding. "No one ever worried about me before either . . . . It takes a while getting used to the idea, but I'm glad you do."

She remained with him until the doctor returned and insisted he get more rest. She went without argument, returning that evening, spending a couple of hours at the hospital along with Karen, Wright's wife, before the two of them went home at around ten. At eleven, just after a nurse had checked to see that the detectives were asleep, Kinnaird made his move. As he climbed out of bed and tottered towards a wardrobe, Wright woke up.

"What're you doing?"

"Going out for a bit. Hold the fort till I get back."

"Are you kidding?"

"I need to talk to Lenny Jones."

"And what's he got to say that hasn't already been said?" Wright pushed himself up on his elbows.

"He saw Hastings, and knew about the redhead. What I didn't ask was whether they visited together, and I've an idea they did."

"Why don't you ask Evans to check it out?"

"I want to do this myself."

"Why? Because you're making this personal. You know it's dangerous when you do something like that." Wright watched Kinnaird pull his clothes out of the wardrobe and unsteadily dress himself. "It's a dumb thing to do in your condition, Del. I'm coming with you!"

"Now that is dumb!" Kinnaird rounded on him. "All I've got is a headache, but you need rest so that you don't spring a leak."

His partner ignored him, climbed out of bed, and pulled the drip feed out of his arm. "I'm going with you, and I'm not arguing about it."

"What if you start bleeding again?"

"You'll save me, just plug the hole with your finger."

"I doubt that'd be big enough."

Wright took a few tentative steps which did not look good, and Kinnaird wished he had taken more care not to have woken him. "Let me worry about me, Del. Now, how're you intending we get out of this place, because after what happened here, they'll have improved security."

"We walk out the front door. There's a payphone in reception, I'll call for a cab from there." Kinnaird watched Wright struggle into his clothes with a growing sense of apprehension. "Y'know, you really don't look good."

"Believe me you're no picture of health either."

They finished dressing in silence, then Kinnaird asked, "How do I look now?"

"Terrible." Wright swayed. "Maybe you should darken your face with polish and pretend you're a Sikh. That band aid on your head looks ridiculous."

"Thanks, pal."

Wright leaned on him for support as they stepped out of the room, his breathing strained, his movements slow, cumbersome, but he wouldn't stop. Kinnaird tried being strong by accepting his partner's weight, but every step was a nightmare, his stomach churned with the effort and his head throbbed like a drum.

"Maybe this wasn't such a good idea," Kinnaird suggested.

"You've had better."

"You want to go back?"

"Only if you do."

"This is dumb."

They kept moving. Fortunately, the exit was not far and the detectives met few staff along the way and none they knew. They concentrated so hard on escaping the hospital they forgot about calling for a cab. Standing outside under a clear night's sky Wright sighed, "Do we go back or what?"

"Or what," Kinnaird replied as he watched an ambulance back up to the casualty entrance. Its crew climbed out, walked to the back doors and helped an elderly woman clamber down. A nurse hurried towards her with a wheel-chair, collected her, swung it round and headed back into casualty. Kinnaird called to the ambulance crew as they closed the back doors, "Hey, are you going to be driving past Fulham nick?"

The crew's eyes widened at the sight of the detectives wobbling towards them. The driver did the talking. "Why? D'you wanna hand yourselves in for stealing bandages?"

Kinnaird forced a smile and hoped that it looked friendly, "We're old bill, just need a lift back to the nick, that's all."

The driver's partner studied Wright, "Is he well enough to be on his feet?"

"I can talk for myself," Wright snapped. "I look a lot worse than I am."

"Glad to hear it. This ain't a hearse, mate."

"How come your own people haven't come to collect you?" The ambulance driver wanted to know.

"I think they're too busy."

"Well you look like you've suffered enough, hop in the back." The driver opened one of the rear doors and the detectives climbed in, relieved as they sat down. Wright looked worse. His eyes were closed as his breath came out in short, raspy sounds while his complexion turned the colour of snow. Kinnaird checked under his jacket for signs of blood loss but found the bandages were clean.

"How're you feeling, Greg?"

"Not good, but I'll be all right in a minute."

The ambulance moved. The station was a ten-minute journey, and each minute Kinnaird scrutinised his partner. When they reached their destination Wright was semi-conscious.

"You can't go on like this, Greg."

"I hate to admit it," he swallowed and it looked painful, "but I think you're right."

Kinnaird climbed out and walked around to the driver's door, "My partner's had a relapse, you'd better rush him back to hospital."

The blue light on the ambulance roof began to flash as the driver U-turned and sped back the way they had come. The detective watched until they disappeared around a corner then trudged passed the police station towards a mini-cab office.

When Kinnaird arrived at Tina Wilson's apartment building the porter acted as if he hadn't noticed the bandages covering most of his head, not that Kinnaird was in a mood to offer an explanation. He used the elevator up to the second floor and gave exercise a rest. Tina Wilson's sister opened the front door on a chain and spoke through a six-inch gap.

Her attitude was terse, "What?"

"I want to talk to Lenny."

"He's out!"

"He's never out, get him to come to the door." She hesitated, glanced behind her but did not move. Her reluctance made Kinnaird angry, "Do you recall who I am?"

"I recall, even with your disguise." She glanced at the bandages.

Kinnaird grimaced, "Get him to the door. Do it now!"

She faltered, glanced up the hall then back to him, "He doesn't want to talk to you, you can't force him."

"I'm coming through this door if he isn't here in ten seconds!"

She chewed nervously on her lower lip, then disappeared leaving the door open on the chain. Kinnaird leaned forward and cocked an ear to hear what was being whispered close by. A moment later Lenny Jones appeared at the gap, looking upset.

"What d'you want man? Ain't you done enough harm to us? They took away Tina's kid, there was no need for 'em to do that."

"Open the door, Lenny."

"Why should I?"

"'Cos I'll kick it in if you don't!"

"You can't come in here without a warrant!"

Kinnaird threw his weight against the door and tore the chain free. The girl screamed and scurried into a bedroom while Jones remained in the hall, naked except for a pair

58

of boxer shorts.

"You didn't have to do that, man."

"I asked you politely to open it," Kinnaird grabbed him by the throat and pushed him against a wall. "These bastards murdered three more people last night, but it could easily have been five, and I might've been one of them. For that reason there are no longer any rules, I want them, that's it!"

"I've told you all I know."

"You're not listening to me, it wasn't enough!" Kinnaird squeezed Jones' neck until his eyes bulged. From somewhere deep within him his strength had returned, perhaps it was anger, whatever, it helped him ignore the throbbing in his skull.

"What else?"

"Hastings and the redhead were together when they came here, weren't they. Is Hastings someone special?" It occurred to Kinnaird that the man calling himself Hastings had taken a lot of trouble keeping his identity secret.

"I don't know nuthin' else."

The detective seethed, his grip tightened and Jones began to turn blue. "I want this scum, Lenny, it's no use you holding anything back!"

Jones coughed, and gestured that he couldn't speak, Kinnaird relaxed his grip. "They're bad people to mix it with, take a look in the mirror if you don't believe me!"

"You're frightened of the wrong people, Lenny. I survived their worst, and in this game no one gets a second chance. Next time we meet I'll be the one handing out the hurt."

"You say, but you're still a cop, and cops follow rules and whatever happens to them won't go beyond that. If they think I helped you I'm a dead man."

Kinnaird swapped his grip around Jones' throat for what

hung between his legs, and squeezed. "But I'm a bad cop, Lenny. You want me to demonstrate just how bad?"

Jones eyes widened further, he did not enjoy being manhandled, especially by someone with a grip like Kinnaird's. "This ain't funny, man."

"Do you see me laughing?" He squeezed a little more and Jones winced. "I could put you out of action for months. What would Tina's sister do then?"

"Please man, don't . . . . "

"Tell me about Hastings and the woman. Tell me everything you know, especially what was said when they came here . . . . together?"

Jones showed no surprise that he had been able to work that much out alone. "I still only saw the man."

"How come?"

"In Tina's bedroom we used to prop up some mirrors. Tall ones because they liked to watch themselves doing things, or at least the man did. The woman always kept her clothes on. I told you that no one could touch her."

"You still haven't answered my question. How come you only ever saw Hastings?" Kinnaird released his lapels and backed away putting a little space between them.

"I was getting to that. I overslept one morning. I was in the other bedroom, Tina thought I was out. I heard them at it and crept along for a look, but I only saw him."

"Why all the secrecy about them coming here?"

"I don't know. Tina told me that was the way they wanted it. She was scared of 'em, I mean really scared. That weren't like her, but I wasn't interested enough to push it further, they paid too well."

"What else?"

He shrugged, "There's a way you might find out more.

60

Tina met them through one of the other girls. I don't know which, it could be any of a dozen."

"Not good enough, Lenny. I need a name. Who'd she regularly share customers with?"

"I can give you a lot of names if you've plenty of paper?"

"Just the most likely ones will do."

"She's been a whore a long time, and she was the friendly kind."

"Follow me." Kinnaird led the way to the bathroom where he washed his hands. Then he took a pen and pad from a pocket and scribbled down a list of twenty names. The last one came as a surprise – Sheenarena. "Some must be more likely than others, which would you say?"

"I can't. It has to be any of 'em."

"The last one's dead."

Jones tottered back against a wall suddenly excited. "You musn't ever let 'em find out that I helped you. They're bad people."

"We already went through that."

"Yeah, and you're still the one with the sore head!"

"Is Hastings the real name for this bloke?" Hastings and the redhead had gone to a lot of trouble keeping their identities secret. It was just possible using an alias was another pre-caution.

"I don't know, honest."

Kinnaird moved into the hall, "You recall anything else, Lenny, contact me at the nick."

"Sure," Jones replied without enthusiasm.

The door slammed shut behind Kinnaird as he headed to the elevator. He felt as if things were finally on the move, and was even beginning to feel better as he stepped outside and met a bitter cold wind visiting the street. He had something to work on now, a distraction that made the pain in his head easier to ignore. He started down the steps to the kerb when two things happened. First, Lenny Jones crashed through one of the second-floor windows and rocketed to the ground head first. Second, Tina's sister followed him. They struck concrete twenty feet from the detective so that he heard the sickening splat of death both times.

Kinnaird turned back to the street door, smashed a glass and was inside headed towards the stairs before the porter came to find out what was happening. The apartment's front door hung open and inside a menacing darkness beckoned. The ache in his head banged as if new but with his adrenalin flowing it was barely a nuisance.

He knocked on the front door of the apartment opposite, and kept knocking until it was answered.

A tall, straight-backed, burly man glared at him with dark, angry eyes. When he spoke it sounded like a gun going off. "What do you want at this hour?"

"There's been a murder in the apartment opposite, call the police, I need help." Kinnaird waved his ID under the man's nose and got an immediate response.

"You think the killer's still in there, eh?" The man's anger turned instantly into curious co-operation.

"There might be a couple of them."

"Betty, call the police, there's been a murder opposite," his voice boomed so loud Kinnaird guessed the entire block must have heard. "I'll give you a hand, officer; haven't had a decent scrap in ages."

Kinnaird did not want to appear unappreciative, but had the feeling that a pair of homicidal maniacs would have the upperhand. After all, he was walking wounded and the man was past his prime.

"Don't worry, son, I'm as fit as a man half my age. Ex-marine commando. If they're inside we'll flush 'em out!" He stepped towards the other apartment without waiting for Kinnaird to follow.

"What the hell," the detective shrugged and stepped in front of the ex-soldier. "OK, Marine, let's take a look."

Kinnaird went ahead, pushed the open door against a wall and searched for a light switch. When the hall light obliterated the darkness the apartment appeared less forbidding. They moved carefully forward, past a couple of open doors until attracted by a sound from one of the rooms facing the street. The ex-marine jumped into a bent knee martial arts posture that showed he hadn't forgotten his training. When nothing happened they rushed into the room and met a bitter wind blowing in through the window that Jones and the girl had gone through, nothing else. A search of the rest of the apartment came up with the same result. Outside the wail of a siren told them help had arrived. Kinnaird thanked the ex-marine, explained that he might be required to provide a statement, and received some gratitude in return simply for the excitement.

Kinnaird was standing beside a patrol car outside Tina Wilson's apartment building when Evans found him. "Why aren't you in hospital?"

"I had more questions for Jones."

"Only someone beat you to it, eh?"

"I got what I wanted. This happened just after I left."

"What did you get?" The DI pulled the collar up on his coat as the wind picked up. He looked tired and irritable. Another couple of murders had been added to a list of dead that appeared like an epidemic, and they were no further into finding those responsible.

"I've the names of twenty other toms who shared customers. One of them shared Hastings and the redhead."

"Give me the list and I'll have them checked out in the morning."

"I was hoping you'd let me do that."

"How can I? You shouldn't even be here. The doc told me that you're unfit for duty. If I allowed you to run around and something went wrong . . . . I'd have an even bigger headache than you!"

It came as a rare experience for Kinnaird to hear Evans talk him out of work. Unfortunately, it was one time when he really wanted to do it. "How about letting me keep the list until I'm fit again?"

"Are you kidding? It's the best lead we've got. It needs to be followed up immediately."

"I'm the one who got it, remember."

"And I thank you for that, but you ain't your own police force, there's a whole bunch of us trying to do the same job! Imagine if these psychos begin knocking off the girls on your list, where're we gonna be then?"

Kinnaird was annoyed, annoyed because he wanted more than anything to find the killers himself, and he was being forced to give away the only lead anyone had. On top of that he knew Evans was right. Reluctantly he handed the list over.

"You know there's no other way, Del. Now get back to the hospital, and next time you get a good idea, call me, don't do anything like this again!"

Kinnaird rode back to the hospital in a patrol car, and surrendered himself to an irate night-duty sister.

THREE

Immediately Kinnaird returned to work, Evans wanted to see him. The DI's office was full of cigar smoke from a thick Havana smouldering in the side of Evans mouth, the threat of cancer not enough to put him off the habit. The tiredness Kinnaird had seen only a few nights ago had totally disappeared; now, the DI looked even sharper than usual. "Glad to have you back, Del. Pull up a chair. I guess you must be wondering how we made out with that list of names?"

"I read the newspapers. You haven't picked anyone up."

"We checked them all except one, and none of those had any recollection of a redhead or Hastings."

"So who's left?"

"A kid called Debbie Ash. Here are her details." He handed Kinnaird a report sheet. It read:

Debbie Ash, date of birth – 2.10.52, place of birth – Fulham. Hair: Blond. Eyes: Blue. Face: Freckled. Height: 5' 2". Build: Medium. Distinguishing Marks: None. Aliases: Saucy Sue, Ready Eddy, Randy Mandy, Belinda Blue.

A photograph came attached which he pulled free. "Can I keep this?"

"Everyone else has one."

Kinnaird finished reading the report. Both her parents were dead, and an address along the Wandsworth Bridge Road in Fulham was recorded as her current residence. It was apparently owned by her aunt, a Mrs Gabrielle Hersey, a widow and known prostitute and brothel-keeper. Debbie Ash had convictions for shoplifting and prostitution since the age of fourteen. Among her known associates were: Tina Wilson, Sarah Bankbird, Veronica Pryce and Angel Gibbon. She was also suspected of operating as a prostitute for Martin Duffy, alias 'The Man'.

"Has anyone interviewed Duffy?"

"I thought I'd save that pleasure for you."

"You did? We're not exactly friends. In fact he tends to throw up whenever he sees me."

"Only because you keep punching his boys out, which makes you the best person to take him a message from me. If we've a gang war in progress I want him to be certain that there aren't going to be any winners, except us."

"I think I can manage that. What about the girl? I take it someone visited her aunt?"

"The aunt's unco-operative, but the gist of a mouthful of abuse suggests that she hasn't seen her niece for several weeks, and couldn't care less about her."

"I'll still pay her a visit, maybe I can charm out of her what others couldn't."

"Good luck, she sounds like a horror to me."

"Is there anything else?" Kinnaird rose from a chair and moved to the door.

"Plenty of dead ends. You haven't missed much these past few days." Evans leaned his elbows on the desk and suddenly looked a little strained. "By the way, I'm handing you a temporary partner till Greg returns. The DCI doesn't want anyone working solo on this."

"Who've you given me?"

"Someone off the Crime Squad. Young and eager, just like

we used to be. Been doing good things I'm told."

"Great, so who is he?"

"An officer called Mowatt."

"Mowatt? What kind of a name's Mowatt?"

"Scots."

"Christ, one drink and they're headcases who want to take on the world."

"I doubt you'll have that problem, she doesn't drink."

"She?" Kinnaird's face screwed up as his eyes turned to narrow slits of horror.

"Melanie Mowatt." The DI blew out a fresh cloud of smoke. "I hope that you're not going to make a big deal out of this, Del."

"Is that right?"

"She's a good kid, a good looker too. Some of the other blokes are green with envy."

"Then give her to one of them, I don't work with women, and you know the very good reason why!"

"That was a long time ago, you should forget it. Take a look at her." Through a glass panel he nodded in the direction of a group of male officers surrounding a female. "She's the one in the red top and skirt. Nice boobs."

Colin Evans never complimented women, they were too high up his list of dislikes because of something to do with a wife and two wild teenage daughters. Thus Kinnaird was immediately suspicious as he stared at the tall, pretty young woman with shoulder-length fair hair. "I don't want to work with her."

"I'm not asking, Del." Evans replied firmly. "She's good, Harry Vickers told me so."

"We're not going out to nick a bunch of shoplifters, and I don't want the repsonsibility of carrying anyone who won't be able to hack it."

"She had eighty-seven crime arrests last year, only one of those was for shoplifting, and that one she caught off duty!"

"How long has she been in the job?" The DI hesitated and looked down at the papers littering his desk. "How long?"

"Almost two years."

"Damn it, she's still a probationer!" Kinnaird returned to Evans' desk, leaned his palms flat on it and met the other man's gaze. "Christ if I've got to take a sprog along, at least make it male!"

The DI rose to his feet. There was a difference of a couple of inches between them, and Kinnaird held the edge. If winning the argument had relied on physical stature alone, Kinnaird would be a winner.

"You've got her, everyone else is already teamed. Make the best of it!"

"Tell me why no one else took her until today?"

"She only just got back from holiday. Now go out and introduce yourself!"

Kinnaird took another look at her, "If she's so good she can start off by finding me!" He left Evans, strode across the office without stopping and stepped into the corridor. As he headed towards the back stairs that led down to the station yard a female voice with a Scot's accent called his name. He stopped and waited for her to join him. She was smiling.

"Del Kinnaird, I'm Melanie Mowatt. Mel to my friends." She offered him a handshake, but he gave her a nod and started down the stairs. "We're supposed to be teamed."

"I know. Have you ever worked on a murder enquiry?"

"This is my first . . . . I was told that you're the best officer to work with on something like this." She sounded cheerful, as if looking forward to their sharing time together. But Kinnaird thought she was being clever, trying to break down his obvious resistance. Everyone in the office knew that he refused to work with women, and didn't doubt someone had enjoyed explaining that to her. Whether anyone bothered explaining his reasons was another matter. "I expect to learn a lot."

When they reached the bottom of the stairs, Kinnaird stopped by the yard door. "This is a rough case, and it's going to get rougher. If I had my way I wouldn't have you along with me, nothing personal."

"They warned me that you've a thing about working with a woman."

"They're right, whoever 'they' are."

"OK, but I guess I was put with you because I'm good."

"At what?" He stepped through the door with her close behind as he headed towards his car.

"Nicking villains."

"So it's not because I'm the best and you're sleeping with the chief super?"

"No, I'm saving him for when I don't want to be your partner."

When they reached the car he faced her. "We need to get a few things straight before this goes any further."

"Obviously."

"First thing you have to understand is that I don't want you as my partner."

"You already said that. What's second?"

"Second is the reason why I don't like working with women. Any I've partnered have been a hindrance. Women slow me down. I need a man as a partner to deal with a tough murder investigation like this. I can't believe Evans would do this to me, I haven't had a female partner in four years."

"Your luck had to run out sooner or later."

Kinnaird ignored her remark along with her smile. "Women need looking after, and if I have to do that while we're working I put my own neck on the line. If you want to work with me, you'll have to make certain you never need my help."

"Heaven forbid."

"Also, you do everything I tell you to do even when you don't think it makes sense."

"Is that rare?"

"You do it without using your own brand of initiative . . . which I'm certain will be hard, but I'm the one with all the experience, and on the streets that's what counts!"

"Is that all?"

"Not quite." He opened the car door, "If you make one mistake while you're with me, you come back here and hide out until this thing's over."

"You've really taken to me, haven't you?" She moved around to the other side of the car, "Thanks for being frank."

"No problem."

As she climbed in beside him she said, "They have names for men like you."

"Realist."

"That isn't one of them." She folded her arms as he started the engine. "I sympathise about what happened to you, but I think I detect that you don't believe in women having the same opportunities as men?"

"You mean the same opportunity of having your throat cut?"

"That doesn't scare me."

"It should, it does me."

"I know what's really bothering you, Kinnaird. You're the same as every other man in this job, scared that a woman might prove to be a better cop than you. I bet I can handle myself as well as you."

"Really, and where'd you learn to box?"

Her chin rose defiantly, "I'm into karate. I'm a First Dan black belt, so you don't have to worry about me complaining that you harassed me. You wouldn't get the chance!"

"And that's the reason you're not scared about getting your throat cut?"

"I'm not."

"Good. You can take my place if we ever get into that kind of trouble."

"I want you to know that I'm not impressed by you Kinnaird. I was expecting . . . " she paused as though lost for the right words.

"You don't have to come with me?"

"I don't have a choice," she glared at him. "I have to obey orders!"

They drove out of the station with Kinnaird wondering what the chances were that she would last more than a day at his side.

The detective drove to the Wandsworth Bridge Road address where Debbie Ash, the last living prostitute on Jones' list, was meant to live. The journey completed in an easy silence, easy because neither wanted to talk. The house was a red-brick, two-storey terraced with a large bay window to the right of the front door. It looked clean and well maintained. A tiny front garden had been laid out in concrete to accom-

71

modate a small car. At the front door sat a large fluffy white cat that seriously should have considered going on a diet. It rose up to greet them and curled itself around Mowatt's legs. She tickled it below the chin and rolled off some unintelligible cat speak. The animal showed its appreciation by dropping on to its side and purring furiously.

"At least *he* likes you," Kinnaird told her.

"He's got taste."

He used the door bell but five minutes later they were still outside with the cat, only now the detective was using a knocker.

"Maybe no one's in?" said Mowatt.

"Someone's in." He nodded towards the bay window. From behind a net curtain a face stared at them.

"Why isn't she answering the door?"

"Maybe she's dead?"

"That isn't funny, Kinnaird."

"They work late here, I guess we got her out of bed." He banged the knocker again.

The face disappeared from the window and a moment later the front door opened. A big woman in her mid-fifties with a vast chest, bleary eyes and sour expression confronted them. She wore a frilly black night gown which finished around her fleshy, white knees, and was probably see through if the light were caught right. Mowatt doubted anyone could be that desperate.

"What d'you want? I've already seen your blokes and told them I don't know where she is!"

"We'd like to talk to Debbie's aunt, Mrs Hersey. Would you get her for us?"

"I am her aunt," the woman frowned.

"Sorry, you didn't look old enough," Kinnaird smiled as

if he meant it. Mowatt took a deep breath and struggled to retain a sharper reply. But the woman had already lost some of her sourness.

"So what d'you want with me?"

"Debbie's life could be in danger, Mrs Hersey," Mowatt said. "We need to find her."

"Like I told the others, I don't know anything."

"Everyone knows something, Mrs Hersey," Kinnaird said as the cat sneaked inside while her owner was distracted.

"Well I don't!"

"We won't go away."

"You can stay out there all day for all I care!"

"We could, but we won't because you're not going to let us."

"I'm not?"

"No, because you want to hear what else we've got to say. It's important."

"If it's that important, say it?"

"Inside, where it's less public."

"The public have never bothered me, the cops have though, but if you're the sensitive kind . . . . maybe this once I won't ask you to get a warrant." She opened the door wider and allowed them into a hall. When she had closed the door she turned to Kinnaird and ignored the female officer. "I really hate cops."

"We all have our idiosyncrasies. Me, I hate treading in dog shit."

The woman smiled, then glanced at Mowatt, looking her up and down, "Are you sure she's a cop?"

"That's what she tells me."

"She'd make a great hooker, nice tits, and that's some mouth. I bet she knows how to use it."

"Take my word for it," Kinnaird stared pointedly at Mowatt's mouth. She glared at him but resisted the urge to say what was on her mind. "I'm certain she'll value your comments, Mrs Hersey."

The woman used a bottom stair as a seat. "We'll stay here, the rest of the place is a tip at the moment. You start whenever you want. I'm all ears."

"We believe that Debbie knows the identities of two killers."

The woman folded her fleshy arms below her huge bosom as if it required a shelf to rest on. "The ones that threw Lenny Jones out of a window?"

"The same."

She snorted and cleared her nostrils, "The girls they've croaked might've mattered, but they did the rest of this planet a favour getting rid of him. Lazy good-for-nothing he was."

"We believe Debbie's lying low until this thing blows over because she knows them." Mowatt interrupted. "If we can find her we can help."

"She always so serious about her job?" The woman asked Kinnaird and received a nod. "What about Debbie, Mrs Hersey?" Mowatt found it impossible to hide the irritation she felt.

"Ease up girl, I'm not that interested in her welfare."

"She's keen," Kinnaird told her. "Has Debbie been living here long?"

"She moved in with me a couple of years ago, but she uses this place like a hotel. I don't try tying her down, it wouldn't work if I did."

"Does she pay her way?"

"When she stays she does. There ain't nothing free in this world." She unfolded her arms and leaned her elbows behind

74

her on a stair. "You're a good-looking fella. Are the two of you at it?"

Mowatt flinched as Kinnaird winked. "We're just good friends."

"Lucky bitch!"

"I agree, but what about Debbie? When do you expect to see her again?"

"How long's a piece of string?" She shifted to one side of the step she was sitting on and patted the space beside her. "Why don't you come and join me here?"

Kinnaird doubted that the two of them would fit, even if he had wanted. "Is there anyone special that she's likely to shack up with?"

"It wouldn't be a bloke." She looked disappointed that he had not joined her. "They're not her scene, except when she needs to earn a few bob." She reached under an armpit and scratched while her face took on a distant, thoughtful expression. "You might try another hooker called Mona. They are the best of pals."

"Where would we find her?"

The hand scratching her armpit disappeared, swallowed up. "She lives over Notting Hill. Check with your blokes there, they're bound to know her. She uses the name Ebony."

"Because she's black?" Mowatt asked.

"What else?" the woman stared at her as if she were an idiot. "She's black as the Ace of Spades. At one time they were inseparable, but I don't know if things are still the same. Debbie's the kind who bores easily."

"Thanks, Gabrielle," Kinnaird grinned. She had given them more than anyone else, and he was grateful.

"So you know my first name," she stared at him as if he had just scored more points in winning her favour.

"It's a nice name."

"You should come back when you're on your own. I look a lot better at night after I've had my beauty sleep. Maybe we could talk over why you made a silly mistake and joined the law?"

Kinnaird nodded, and noticed Mowatt staring at the woman as if she agreed about her looking better at night. "I'll bear that in mind."

"I hope you do."

Mowatt stepped outside and returned to the car without uttering another word to either of them. Kinnaird thanked the woman again before joining her.

As he climbed in behind the wheel he glanced at Mowatt. "At least she thought you had nice . . . . "

"Don't say it, Kinnaird," she growled through gritted teeth. "I've had just about enough of you for one day without you adding anything more. Consider yourself lucky that I'm able to control my temper."

"I was only going to agree with what she said about your mouth." He laughed and enjoyed seeing her blush. "Would you like me to drop you off at the nick?"

She turned slowly to face him, her eyes ablaze. "I told you that I've been ordered to stay with you, and that's what I'm doing!"

"You don't have to do anything that doesn't suit you, especially if you're finding it too tough. I'll help if you want to be partnered to someone else?"

"You'd like me to do that, wouldn't you? Then you could crow about how I didn't have what it takes to be your partner, but I have, and I'm staying!"

"You must like me, even if it's only a little bit?"

"I think I hate you, and I think it's a lot!"

He shrugged and turned the ignition key. "Anyway, cheer up. I can't stand having a misery for a partner."

"Oh, sorry, but it's tough being a bag of laughs when you're with a moron!" It came out of her so sweetly that he almost mistook it for a compliment.

"It's a tough life, kid."

"Christ, is that how you try coming across as the big I am, by calling female officers, kid? Well I'm not a kid, and you better remember that!"

"So how old are you?" He reminded himself that he had been hard on her, that it wasn't her fault that they had been teamed together. Yet there was something about her which seemed to goad him into teasing her, which made him want to make her angry. He found whatever it was irresistible.

She shook her head, "Twenty-two, and don't try selling me any crap about how young that is for this job."

"I won't. A year on the streets as a cop teaches you more about life than ten years in any office job, but you've still a few things to learn. For example, leave the talking to the officer who's getting the right responses. Back there that was me."

"I was trying to help, all she was interested in was your body, and I couldn't imagine even you surrendering to that!"

"You should know that every woman likes to think they're sexy, it's human."

"You certainly played her along, I wouldn't be surprised if she calls up the film studios and asks to play a part reserved for Raquel Welch. Or is it simply that you've a thing about fat old bags? Nothing would surprise me where you're concerned."

"As I said, you've still things to learn." He idly wondered what she would say when she found out that Vienna was almost twelve years his junior. It troubled him that she might make too much of it, that he might lose his temper if she did.

"You're full of wind, Kinnaird."

"OK, let's call a truce. I've been pretty hard on you, I admit it, but we'd better stop this thing now."

"I want to prove to you that I'd be as good as you in a fight, maybe even better. Why don't we stop somewhere so that I can give you a demonstration?"

"If you were a man I'd take you up on that, but you're not, and I'm not into beating up women!"

"Frightened that I might win?"

"If I were you, I'd shut it down right now!"

"I'd rather you pulled into an alley, but if you don't have the nerve . . . . " she left the rest unsaid.

"Say I did, how'd I then explain your broken arm, jaw or leg?"

She rounded on him with a snarl, "Listen, Kinnaird, I trained damn hard to get my black belt at karate just so that I could punch holes in people like you. Oh, you're big, but that doesn't amount to much when you're up against someone who knows what she's doing!"

He couldn't believe his ears, couldn't believe that she could be so naïve. "You and me are a no contest. I was a semi-pro heavyweight for several years. I weigh more than two hundred pounds, and bench press over three hundred. What I can do to punch bags would make you wish you never opened your mouth!"

"Keep talking tough, Kinnaird, if that's what makes you feel like a man, but we both know better!"

"A few years ago I had a chance to become a professional heavyweight, do you have any idea what that means?"

"That you're scared of being beaten by a woman?"

"Lady, you're tempting me."

"I doubt it. Think what it would mean to your prestige if I won, you'd be finished as a tough guy."

It was Kinnaird's turn to feel angry. Angry at himself for allowing her to goad him, to make him feel as if he had something to prove. Damn it, she was the probationer! He glanced at her and spotted an insolent smugness in her eyes. She was enjoying herself. Pleased that she had found a chink in his armour. Perhaps even surprised that it had been so easy – it had certainly surprised him. He sighed, "If you can handle yourself as well as you say, that's good for me to know."

"Does it mean you don't mind having me as a partner?"

"No. It means I'll need to watch you even more. You're the type to try doing something heroic. It's a good job you're nice to look at, makes watching you less of a hardship."

"And I thought you were fond of your girlfriend, but like every other man, all you think about is either brawling or sex with very little in between. For a while I actually thought you'd be different."

"What are your vital statistics?"

"Why should I tell you?"

"No real reason. I was simply trying to maintain our conversation at a level you think appropriate for me."

"Do you act this way with every woman you work with?"

"I told you, I don't work with women."

"I think you've got that wrong, women probably won't work with you!"

"Tell me something, and this is serious. Why don't you like being a woman?"

"What are you going to say next, Kinnaird, that I'm a dyke?"

"You're trying too hard to compete with men. That's what all this karate nonsense is about. You think if you go around knocking out every hardcase you meet you'll turn into one yourself. Well I've news for you, being a hardcase isn't tough, but being who you really are, is. You might do better if you concentrated on the latter."

"Thanks for the free analysis."

They remained silent until they drove into the carpark at the Roma Restaurant in Fulham Road.

"In case you're wondering. We're here to visit – The Man."

"Martin Duffy."

"You've heard of him."

"Any officer worth their salt has heard of him," she replied disdainfully.

"So tell me what you know?"

"He runs the biggest vice operation this side of the river, which probably means he's into all other forms of crime including drugs, though it's never been proved."

"Well done."

"I haven't finished. Three of his girls have been attacked so far, but Sheenarena is the only one who wound up dead."

"Good, but you haven't mentioned Debbie Ash?"

"I didn't know they were connected."

"Didn't you see the sheet Colin Evans supplied?"

"I haven't had a chance. I only reported back from holiday this morning. That's when I was told about us being teamed up, just before you walked out of the office. You know the rest."

"It's suspected that Debbie worked for him. I don't know if she still does, but I do know that he likes to keep tabs on those that have. It's a form of insurance on his income."

"Does he own the restaurant?"

"No, just lives in it." They climbed out of the car and used a side entrance to get into the restaurant.

The cleaning staff were there vacuuming while a couple of barmen stocked shelves behind a counter. Kinnaird led her over to the counter, "We're looking for Duffy."

Neither barman stopped working, "He ain't here."

"He's always here at this time of day. Get him on the blower and tell him Del Kinnaird wants to talk to him."

The barmen stopped stocking shelves and looked up. One was about six feet tall and well muscled. The sleeves of his shirt rolled up so his large biceps were obvious beneath a dozen tattooes. The other one had less of everything but looked wiry and held a bottle by its neck. The taller of the two said, "And who the fuck is Del Kinnaird when he's at home?"

"The person who's going to rearrange your face unless you do as you're told!" Evans had been right about him picking fights with Duffy's men whenever he got the chance, but what he really wanted was a crack at Duffy himself. The barmen came out from behind the counter and Kinnaird sensed Mowatt tense. He idly wondered what she was thinking, and if she had ever used her karate expertise for real.

"Don't you think you should ask us who we are before you do something you're likely to regret?"

The tall one spoke again, "We know who he is, he just told us. He's the bloke who's gonna try and rearrange my face."

"Ask him what he does for a living," she urged.

"You mean apart from acting tough. OK, impress us, what d'you do?"

"What I do, shithead, is be a cop!"

81

"Wot,"er an' all?" The wiry one asked, incredulous.

"Believe it, boys." Mowatt showed them her ID.

They looked her up and down before the tall one added, "Nice mouth."

Something passed between her and Kinnaird before he replied, "She's not interested in compliments. Now get Duffy."

"He doesn't like to be disturbed this early. He works late, see." Some of their aggression had subsided, though the tall one still seemed curious to know if the detective was as tough as his mouth suggested.

"Either you fetch him or we'll go find him."

"All right, lads, I'll see to this." Duffy had risen early. As he approached them wearing a friendly smile, the barmen retreated behind the counter. "It's meant to be a time of goodwill to all men, Kinnaird. Let's use one of the tables. Would you like a coffee or perhaps something stronger?"

"No, thanks. We're not interested in being poisoned." They sat at the nearest table and Duffy eyed Mowatt with sneaking respect.

"You shouldn't say things like that when you've a pretty friend with you. She might get the wrong idea about me."

"From the way your eyes undressed her I'd say she doesn't need me as your character referee."

Duffy grinned, his eyes fixed on Mowatt. She returned his smile, and Kinnaird wondered whether she found him attractive, apparently women did. The vice king was in his mid-forties with a mop of thick, curly, dark hair, and steely brown eyes. He had gained a few pounds since they had last met, but he couldn't be called overweight. Duffy trained regularly and had once been a fair boxer before an eye injury had messed up his chances of going further. Because he was around five feet nine, the extra weight gave him a square, barn-doorish appearance.

"We're looking for one of your girls," Kinnaird said.

"Why, when you've such a pretty partner?" Duffy kept his attention focused on Mowatt, who didn't show any signs that she minded.

"We think she's in danger, Mr Duffy," Mowatt's tone was soft, friendly.

He leaned towards her, "If any of my girls have trouble, I take care of it."

"You haven't done too well lately," Kinnaird added and made a point of leaning forward between them.

"You mean the scum who hit Sheenarena?"

"Sheenarena and a few others. So why don't you tell us what's going on?"

"How should I know?" He shrugged and dragged his eyes away from Mowatt. "There's a couple of freaks on the street who hate women and cops. I heard you and Wright got damaged at the hospital. I'd like to have seen that."

"I bet. They were lucky. Next time we meet luck won't have anything to do with it." Kinnaird came forward on his elbows. "But the big trouble is with you. These freaks aren't attacking just any women, they're attacking yours!"

"Tina Wilson wasn't one of mine," Duffy corrected, glanced at Mowatt then back to Kinnaird. "So what are you doing about it?"

"Searching for Debbie Ash."

"Why her?"

"We think she knows them, that she passed them on to Tina."

"She doesn't work for me anymore. She got involved with someone south of the river, that was the last I heard."

"Mona . . . . Ebony?" Mowatt asked.

Duffy smiled and focused his attention on the police-woman, "Not Mona Curtis. She lives in Notting Hill. Debbie went off with a thing called Sonny Fisher, an it."

"Why an it?"

"It's a gender-bender, no one really knows whether it's male or female." His hand moved across the table and rested on top of the female officer's.

"We've been told that Debbie's a lesbian, so I suppose Fisher must be female."

"It wears women's clothes," Duffy sneered, and stroked her hand gently, almost as if hoping she wouldn't notice. "To my mind it's still a bloke in drag. It's big, broad and struts around just like the apes that work for me."

Kinnaird was agitated by Duffy touching his colleague's hand, and by her for allowing him to do it.

"I know some women who fit that description."

"Listen Kinnaird, I'm trying to help you, which is more than usual." The vice king didn't look at him, focusing on Mowatt while his hand grew bolder caressing up to her wrist.

"Who is Fisher? Why did Debbie go with him?" If what Duffy was doing bothered her, it didn't show.

"I'm told he's big in the south's flesh traffic."

"Competition?" Kinnaird shifted uneasily.

"Not over here," Duffy laughed, at last distracted by the detective. "He came across once looking to steal some girls. They don't have as many white whores in Lambeth nowadays. He took a hammering for his trouble and all I lost was one."

"Debbie Ash?" Mowatt added.

"You catch on real quick, beautiful."

"Where can we find Fisher?" Kinnaird clamped a hand

around Duffy's wrist, and yanked his hand off Mowatt.

The vice king's eyes grew dark and for a moment Mowatt thought war had been declared. Then the tension subsided as if it had never been, the menace disappeared and Duffy sat back, seemingly unruffled. "Lambeth."

"Be more specific." Kinnaird refused to release him as he tried to twist free.

"You're pushing it, Kinnaird!"

"With you it'll always be to the limit. Whereabouts in Lambeth?"

"Y'know I saved your bacon today, those blokes behind the bar are pretty useful."

"I've been thinking about that. You guessed why we were here, and you want our help, need it. These hits are starting to hurt your business, and you can't stop them."

There was no way of knowing if Kinnaird had guessed right, and Duffy was not about to agree, but he did help. "Brixton, that's the best I can offer."

"How long ago did Debbie go over to Fisher?" Mowatt asked coolly, hoping to dispel some of the tension.

"What the hell is a peach like you doing in the old bill, and with an ape like him?"

"Getting an education about slime like you!" Kinnaird wrenched hard on his wrist so the vice king winced. "Now, answer her question!"

Duffy's complexion turned a bright shade of red while his voice became a low, threatening whisper, "No one talks to me like that. No one!"

"I do, and if you really want to impress the lady you'll answer the question before I get mad and punch you to hell!"

Duffy seethed silently but visibly for a full sixty seconds, until he managed to get his temper under control. "We've never really tested that theory about your abilities where I'm concerned."

"Some things people don't need demonstrated. Me taking you apart is one of them!"

"Keep praying I never choose to find out."

"You pray, I'll be here."

"When did you last see Debbie, Mr Duffy?" Mowatt asked the question so sweetly it was as if she had missed everything that had erupted between them.

He told her. Kinnaird guessed that he was not included in their conversation because the vice king didn't look his way as he told her. "About six months ago."

"Did you ever try getting her back?" Kinnaird backed his question with another yank of his wrist.

"Why should I?"

"Because that's the kind of thing you do when people let you down, and she did let you down, didn't she?"

"I'm not interested in her. We had an arrangement and she broke it, that's the finish of it. Sonny Fisher can have her. She'll never work this side of the river again."

"You expect me to believe that?" Kinnaird released him, leaving a deep, red mark where his grip had been.

"This may come as a surprise to you, Kinnaird, but I don't give a damn what you believe. I've told you all I know. If she or Fisher come over here again I'll deal with them, the same way that I'm going to deal with whoever's hitting my girls."

"So they are causing you problems?" Mowatt smiled quizzically, detached from what went on between him and Kinnaird.

"Everything causes me problems, beautiful, it's that time of year. We've lousy weather, a pair of psychos on the loose, and Kinnaird, but we're coping. I intend having a happy Christmas, and an even happier New Year."

"Do you think these attacks are related to someone wanting to muscle in on your business?" she smiled pleasantly, and leaned towards the vice king oozing sex appeal.

"Around here? Are you kidding?" he laughed.

Kinnaird sighed, "You've been kingpin a long time, Duffy. Maybe someone besides me thinks it's too long?"

"Don't get the idea because I resist taking you apart that that goes for anyone else," he scoffed. "I can swat any rivals, but the trouble with this business is that it attracts freaks like flies, and they ain't as easy to find. That's why I want the law to handle it, if they can."

"You could be more helpful if you really wanted to see it sorted, Fisher's address would be a start?"

"Forget it, Kinnaird, you're paid to be a detective, so go detect!"

"It's in your interests that we find Debbie Ash."

"Sure it is. That's why I've just spent the last ten minutes talking to you. Believe me it wasn't because I enjoy your company!" He leaned back on the chair and glanced at Mowatt, "You're different."

"Why don't you tell her where Fisher lives?"

"I don't like being referred to as slime or anything else that you've handed out in the past, but more than that, I really don't like you!"

"I'm gutted."

"Just this once I'm going to give you a chance to come up with a result, if you don't I'll deal with it!"

"If bodies begin appearing we'll know where to come."

"Come with proof or else you'll be talking to my brief about harassment!"

87

Kinnaird rose from the chair, their conversation at an end. Mowatt said goodbye and followed the detective towards the exit. When they climbed into the car she was grinning.

"You've a funny way of getting people to co-operate, Kinnaird. Calling him names isn't the kind of technique to obtain the best results."

"But holding his hand is?"

"It would have been if you hadn't kept interrupting. After all didn't I hear you say, not so very long ago, to leave the talking to the officer getting the right responses?"

"By that I didn't mean that you had to drop your knickers for him. There are limits!"

"Either take that back, Kinnaird, or you've got a fight on your hands!" Her face flushed with anger. The vice king had played up to her, guessing it would irritate Kinnaird, and she had gone along with it to obtain the information they wanted. His criticism of her actions suddenly sounded unfair even to his own ears.

"I apologise," he snapped, hating to admit that he had been wrong and Duffy right. The vice king's familiarity with her had been an affront to their authority. It was also something Kinnaird took as a personal offence. If Mowatt had known him better she would have realised that, and probably withdrawn her hand rather than let it continue.

"I'll give you some advice about Duffy, Kinnaird. Pray that he never forgets you're a cop. He looks mean enough to hand out plenty of pain when he puts his mind to it."

He looked at her, the earlier anger replaced by something less hostile. Relief that she hadn't made a big thing out of his apology. "That's part of the fun of being me, I don't have to worry about slime like Duffy."

"Damn sure of yourself, aren't you?"

"Damn sure." He pushed the gear shift into drive and the Ford rumbled across the carpark towards the exit.

"How come Duffy lives at the restaurant?"

"He's knocking off the owner's wife."

"Where's the owner while that's going on?"

"Abroad. Apparently he only returns to the UK twice a year. He's a workaholic who has businesses around the globe. The story is that he thinks a divorce would cost him too much."

"I really don't understand why some people bother getting married," she glanced at the detective as if waiting to hear his opinion.

"Most do it for the right reasons, you know . . . . love."

"Were you one of those, Kinnaird?"

"How did we swing this round to me?"

"Rumour has it that you used to play around when you were married. I'm just curious why you bothered in the first place if she couldn't hold your attention?"

"We were both young and it was an adventure. When you're twenty and make a lifetime pledge you don't really understand the kind of commitment you're getting yourself into. It's that simple."

"Is that why you haven't married your girlfriend, because you think she's too young?"

"Suddenly you know an awful lot about me?" Kinnaird had been concerned what she might say about his relationship with Vienna. He didn't want to share time with a partner who ridiculed him, even if she did so behind his back. A partner's opinion about him was important, to Kinnaird it measured how much reliance he could place on that person. He knew several officers thought him insane for living with the daughter of a woman who had murdered his wife, and attempted to do the same to him. Their age difference was something else a few had found hard to accept. At the beginning he had been the same, before he had fully grown to love Vienna. Now it mattered less, but it did still matter.

"My reasons for not getting married are exclusively my own."

"Sorry, I didn't mean to be so nosy."

"Yeah."

They drove to Notting Hill police station and spoke to the collator to find an address for Mona Curtis, alias Ebony. The Collator knew Curtis and found her details in his card index without wasting time. Kinnaird copied down her address and thanked him for his help, then was warned to be careful as she had a history of violence.

Mona Curtis lived in a poor part of Notting Hill, in a four-storey, Victorian terraced house converted into one-bedroomed apartments. Most of the houses in the block appeared run down, and could easily have reached the local council's condemned list, but for the moment they were survivors, like the people in them. Kinnaird and Mowatt navigated around a pile of plastic rubbish bags in the front garden, and used a door bell with the name Curtis alongside it. They didn't hear a ring, but someone charged down a staircase and gave them hope. The front door opened and a man rushed out, brushing passed them as if they weren't there. Kinnaird caught the door before it slammed shut and led the way inside. Depressing was a good word to describe what they found. The dilapidation was worse inside than out, stains of rising damp were visible on every wall, while a musty stench polluted the air.

"Nice," Mowatt remarked.

They climbed the stairs to the second floor where Mona Curtis lived, and Kinnaird used a fist to bang on the door.

A sound from inside told them someone was home, but no one answered. Kinnaird tried again and received the same response, nothing.

"Time to use section 519," he grinned. Mowatt looked puzzled. His shoulder slammed against the door and it flew inwards bounced against a wall and remained open. Mona Curtis was inside, but only her top half was visible behind a single bed turned on to its side as a shield. A shotgun rested on top of it pointed at Kinnaird's chest. "Police."

"Prove it!" The shotgun shook against the bed as Curtis stared at them with terrified eyes. The detective moved a hand slowly to an inside jacket pocket and pulled out his ID, then threw it on the floor in front of her. "That means nuthin'. There's no picture just words, and the bitch with you doesn't look like a cop!"

Mowatt stood just behind Kinnaird and reached towards a back pocket on her jeans, but she was nervous and did so too quickly. The shotgun twitched in the woman's hands.

"Slowly," Kinnaird told her.

"You listen to him, sister!" Curtis agreed. Mowatt forced herself to be calm and her ID joined Kinnaird's on the floor. "They could both be duff!"

"They ain't," Kinnaird told her. "We're from Fulham CID. We're searching for Debbie Ash and were told Mona Curtis might know where we could find her?"

"Well you found Mona, but Debbie ain't here, and I can't help no more than that!"

"That's a shame because we think Debbie's in danger. We were told the two of you were an item. We were hoping because of that you'd want to help."

"Who'd wanna hurt Debbie?"

Kinnaird took a couple of steps forward and to his right

so that he put some distance between himself and Mowatt. "A couple of killers are knocking off toms, we think Debbie can identify them."

"You stop moving around, man, cop or not I'll give you both barrels if you try somethin'."

"Why the armoury, Mona?"

"This ain't a safe neighbourhood, or hadn't you noticed?"

"I didn't think anyone needed to barricade themselves in behind a shooter."

"It's Debbie's bloody fault I'm like this. The greedy little cow got herself well-in with a bloke who's loaded."

"That doesn't explain why you're in hiding?"

"Her new beau's a jealous bastard. He knows she still loves me. He's frightened I could take her away."

"He?" Mowatt remained by the door, her throat dry, yet outwardly calm. "Debbie's aunt told us she's a lesbian."

"She is. The guy she's with is a freak, but a wealthy one. She's so hung up on having plenty of dosh she left me. I still can't believe it, even though I know what she's doing – spending his money like it's Christmas every day."

"Look, do you mind if I sit down?" Kinnaird glanced at a weathered armchair.

Curtis nodded, "Help yourself."

"Is Sonny Fisher the freak, Mona?" Mowatt held her attention while Kinnaird dropped his behind into the chair.

"It don't matter. What does is that he's sending company. Get inside out of the doorway, close the door, and stand by the wall." She watched Mowatt step into the room and edge left along the wall for a few feet. "That's far enough. Now, who did these killers you're looking for murder?"

"Six people that we know about, Sheenarena, Tina Wilson, her sister, Lenny Jones . . . . "

"Jones was a waste of space!"

"So people keep telling us," Kinnaird said. "But murdering him was still a crime. They also killed a sister at a hospital and a young copper."

"And that makes it worse, does it?"

"Read it how you like, I just want to reach Debbie ahead of them."

"Man take it from me, you ain't got nuthin' to worry about. They'd never get within fifty feet of that girl. I know I tried. Fisher has her safe in his back pocket with round-the-clock company."

"We could help you, Mona. If you'd let us?"

"Forget it. I wouldn't trust this black skin to no cop!"

"We can protect you, that has to be better than this."

"No way. Man, I have a gun."

"But are you dumb enough to use it, look at yourself. You're scared shitless, watching the clock, waiting to die."

"It ain't dyin' that's worrying me, it's what Fisher said they'd do to me." She rose to her feet. She wore a yellow T-shirt that was only baggy around the waist; a huge chest kept it that way. "He said they'd cut off my titties. If I lose them I might as well be dead, they're my biggest asset!"

"I won't argue you with you there, Mona," Kinnaird agreed, and received a disapproving look from Mowatt.

"That's even more reason for us to help you."

Her head shook, "I can't."

He rose slowly from the chair and moved towards her, "Use your head, Mona. You've got serious trouble. Waiting here to die is not the answer. Come with us."

"Don't make me use this, man!" The shotgun wobbled nervously in her hands.

"You've more sense than that. Kill me and you'll go inside

till your hair turns grey. You're a good-looking woman. Don't waste it. We can and will take care of you."

Curtis hesitated, and for a moment Kinnaird thought she would hand him the shotgun, but the door flew open instead. Instinct threw the detective at Mowatt, and they hit the floor just before the shotgun blasts tore the air to shreds. Someone screamed and crashed down beside them whilst someone else let fly with a pistol. When the shooting stopped, Kinnaird rose quickly to his feet and found a black man making a mess on the floor from a hole in his chest while Mowatt clung desperately to the throat of another. The second waved a pistol in the air attempting to line it up on Curtis as Mowatt struggled with him. Curtis screamed and ducked behind the upturned bed. Kinnaird smashed a fist into the man's face and he and Mowatt went down on the floor with a bang. He collected the pistol off the floor while Mowatt climbed out from beneath the inert body and dusted herself down. Behind them Curtis screamed.

"I said you couldn't protect me!" The shotgun waved unsteadily in her hands, not pointing at anyone in particular. "They're gonna cut off my tits! They're gonna cut off my tits!"

"We just helped stop them doing that." Kinnaird moved towards her, but her head shook and he again found himself staring into the double barrels.

"Stay back, I'm getting out of here, and you're not coming with me!"

"Don't be stupid, Mona." Mowatt joined Kinnaird's side. Behind them one of the men scrambled to his feet and ran out of the room before anyone could stop him. Meanwhile Curtis came out from behind the bed, the shotgun levelled at Kinnaird's stomach. "You only get two shots with that thing, Mona, and you've used both."

94

"I reloaded it while you were busy, now get out of the way."

"You didn't have time." He grabbed the barrels and twisted the shotgun free as the hammers clicked home.

Curtis fell on her knees, cradled her head in her hands, and sobbed. "They'll get me. You won't be able to stop 'em."

Kinnaird turned to Mowatt who suddenly looked very pale. "Take care of her, I'm going to use the payphone outside to get some help." She nodded, he moved towards the doorway and paused, "By the way, don't be shy about using your karate if she gets her second wind."

Curtis looked up momentarily then sobbed even louder.

Detective Inspector Colin Evans was not a happy man. People were dying in Fulham and nobody was closer to discovering the identity of the killers. On top of that Kinnaird had asked to go out armed. Asking for a thousand pounds a week might have been easier. The DI puffed on a thick Havana while Kinnaird and Mowatt sat opposite his desk as he pondered their next move. "We need a result, Del, and we need it soon. I'm being hammered by the brass because of all the bad publicity this thing's generating. People are scared and beginning to ask whether we can handle it."

"We're not simply dealing with a couple of nutters, no matter what Duffy wants us believe. This is gang-orientated. Tina Wilson was murdered because she could identify the killers, the same goes for her pimp and sister, but smack in the middle are the north and south vice rackets." Kinnaird covered the conversation they had had with Duffy, including Sonny Fisher and his connection with Debbie Ash and Mona Curtis.

"You might be right," Evans conceded, still harbouring

doubts. "Word on the streets is that every tom working for Duffy wants individual protection, and even The Man can't come up with that. I just wish we had more to go on, because I still can't completely discount that we're only dealing with a couple of crazies, that's how the DCI sees it, by the way. Until we've more proof that you're right about a gang war you'll have to play that angle on your own. Finding Debbie Ash might help answer a few questions. If she knew that we had Mona, she might even come to the station to try and help her. Mona said she still loved her?"

"She loves money more, otherwise she wouldn't be with Fisher."

"Damn crazy world." Evans said flatly, shaking his head. "Lesbians, gays, bisexuals, they're all bloody mixed up."

"Liberated," Mowatt corrected.

"Liberated." He made the word sound like a crime and took the cigar out of his mouth. "The meaning of that word's been twisted to provide a sanctuary for every misfit there is, that's why there's an annual rise in sexually transmitted diseases. Men going with men and women going with women isn't natural. You don't see animals getting it wrong, they've got more sense!"

"It's been happening a long time."

"That doesn't make it right, Del!" He jammed the cigar back in his mouth as they rose from the chairs. Nothing and nobody was going to change the way Evans looked at the world. As far as he was concerned, as a police officer he had witnessed too many grim scenes committed by unnatural offenders to believe only a minority from a minority group became criminals. A God-fearing Catholic, he had a constant struggle to conceal his contempt for those who didn't fit neatly into his idea of society. At the top of his long list of undesirables came homosexuals and lesbians. Kinnaird knew that, as did most of the other officers at Fulham. Evans made a point of telling them so whenever he got drunk, at least twice a week.

As they stepped out of the DI's office Mowatt whispered, "Are there any groups of people he does like?"

"Cops, but sometimes I'm not even sure about them."

Clements, the CID clerk, caught Kinnaird by the arm, "I'm ready to begin a new game whenever you are?"

"I need to powder my nose," Mowatt said, and headed towards the corridor.

Kinnaird allowed himself to be led across the office to where Clements had a chessboard set up. The clerk was full of praise for a book he had recently studied showing easy strategies to win chess games. They had time for three moves each before Mowatt returned, and heard the clerk growl about not expecting Kinnaird to have done something with his queen.

Kinnaird led Mowatt to the station yard. Outside, the sun showed a distant face between layers of thin cloud, managing to raise the temperature a few degrees. They headed towards Kinnaird's Ford Capri with Mowatt looking puzzled, "I thought you wanted to interrogate Mona?"

"Later, first I want her to spend a little solitary time thinking things over."

"So what's the plan now?"

"We eat."

"You mean you actually don't mind being seen eating with me?"

"You did quite well this morning, a prisoner got away at Mona's, but these things happen."

"Careful Kinnaird, that almost sounded like a compliment. Though I knew I'd get the blame for that gunman getting away."

"At the time he was your responsibility, but don't let that ruin our meal." They climbed into the car and he slid the key into the ignition.

"You scared the life out of me when you took that shotgun away from her," she avoided his gaze as she said it. "You couldn't have been certain that she hadn't reloaded it?"

"Call it an educated gamble."

"It was cool."

"Do you have any preferences about what you eat?" The sound of her admiration made him uncomfortable; in many ways life was easier when they were arguing.

"No, I'm easy."

"That's not what I asked."

She glanced at him and shook her head. "I thought we were discussing food?"

"We'll go Italian."

"Sounds romantic. Promise me it isn't going to be like that."

"You have my word."

They had lunch at a pasta house beside Fulham Broadway tube station, where he was welcomed as a friend. They avoided talk about work or people associated with the job and kept conversation to neutral topics. Sid James had died in April while Stanley Baker had followed soon after in June. It turned out that they were fans of both celebrities and were able to discuss performances of either one. When that dried up their conversation moved on to boxing. That year Alan Minter had just hung on to the British middleweight championship against Kevin Finnegan. Both had watched the fight and shared the view that Minter had been lucky.

At three they returned to the station. Kinnaird gave Mowatt the opportunity to interrogate Mona Curtis while he acted like a shadow in a corner of the cell. Curtis was scared of Fisher and reluctant to talk. On top of that Debbie appeared to have let her down, causing her more pain than anything Fisher might have done.

"Look, Mona, whatever you think she's done, she really needs our help." Mowatt paced the floor while Curtis sat on a bench watching her.

"I can't say nuthin'!"

"Why not?"

"Sonny Fisher wouldn't be impressed havin' the bill makin' house calls. If he thought I told you where to find her it'd make him mad as hell. I'm in enough trouble."

"Is Fisher trying to muscle in on Duffy's territory?"

"I ain't sayin'."

"Do you still love her, Mona?" Kinnaird stepped out of the shadows. Curtis shrugged. "You told us that she loves you?"

"Maybe I was wrong," she replied unhappily.

"When did you last see her?"

"A week ago." She stared down at the floor while reliving the moment. "He caught us in my car the last time. Dragged me out by the hair before punching the shit out of me. I mean he can really use his fists, I couldn't fight him off. Then Debbie got between us and I got away."

"Have you spoken to her since?"

"On the phone for a couple of minutes. She told me to forget her. After what happened this morning I guess she meant it."

"Do you think she knew Fisher sent those men after you?"

"She's livin' with him, ain't she."

"That doesn't mean she knew. You could be making a mistake." Mowatt sounded sympathetic. "If Fisher wasn't around, do you think Debbie would come back to you, Mona?"

"She'd have less of a reason to stay away, but he ain't goin' nowhere."

"We could make him disappear if you'd help us. Those goons he sent this morning, if you made a statement telling us that you believed him responsible, we could pick him up."

"It'd be my word against his?"

"It would start out that way, but once we've got him here who knows what might happen? Besides, with him banged up Debbie would be free to join you again. At least the two of you would be able to talk things over without worrying about Fisher."

"Would I need to go to court?"

"Depends on whether or not Fisher pleads to hiring the goons."

"He won't plead to nuthin'. What about the one I killed this morning? Will they put me inside?"

"Self-defence, we're witnesses, leave it to us to sort out. We may need to hold you for a few hours, but that's all." Kinnaird stood over her gauging the moment to push a little more. "Help us find Debbie. I think you'd be upset if anything happened to her and you could have helped prevent it."

Curtis looked up, her eyes watery.

FOUR

Mona Curtis did not have an address for Debbie Ash, but knew that she worked as a "main bitch" for Sonny Fisher between four and five every afternoon at a grocery stall in Brixton Market, operating on his behalf collecting the returns from his string of prostitutes. Thanks to the photograph supplied by the inspector, it did not take them long to find her, even amongst a throng of Christmas shoppers. Short, blond hair, slim build, she wore a pair of jeans beneath a heavy coat with a money pouch tied around her waist. At first they thought that the minder she was meant to have had deserted, then spotted a heavily built black man sitting on a box crate behind her stall, absorbed in a comic.

Brixton had a reputation for public disorder whenever the police attempted an arrest where the public congregated. For that reason Brixton's police management usually sent in an army of officers when they wanted someone collected from amongst a crowd. Kinnaird was aware of that but didn't want the army. He wanted to pick up Debbie Ash as quickly and as quietly as possible. Believing that any show of force would reduce their chances of success, he decided not to warn the local station that he and Mowatt were on their ground.

They split up and approached Ash from two sides, mingling with the crowd and waiting until she was free, her minder still distracted by his comic. Mowatt spoke to her alone, briefly. Mona had told them what to say. Kinnaird remained nearby, standing in front of another stall, watching the young blonde's reaction. Ash screamed, pushed Mowatt away and ran towards the High Street. At about the same time her minder stopped living in fantasy land and jumped off the box crate. Ash rushed through the shoppers and passed Kinnaird while Mowatt vanished in the opposite direction. Like everyone else, Kinnaird looked startled by the commotion. The minder raced after Ash but concentrated too hard on her slim back and missed the foot the detective stuck out in front of him. The man stumbled head first, arms waving to catch his balance, and almost survived, but the same foot kicked his behind and sent him sprawling to the ground. When Kinnaird reached the High Street, his Ford was there with its passenger door open, Mowatt behind the wheel, Ash in the back. He jumped in and the V6 engine roared, the Capri burnt rubber all the way to the traffic lights, sailed through a red, received abuse from the cross-flow traffic stream, and all without Mowatt batting an eye.

"Who are you?" Ash wanted to know as she settled down on the back seat.

"Friends of a friend," Kinnaird replied.

"She never mentioned you before?"

"Don't worry about it."

"Where is she?" The blonde came forward between the front seats to get a better look at them. "I heard Sonny had a contract out on her, but by the time I found a phone to warn her she'd gone."

"They almost got her this morning, but she's safe now."

"You're the bill aren't you?"

He turned and rested an arm on the back of the seat,

"What gave us away?"

"You're not difficult, you're eyes don't stop working, but then your friend threw me. She, I could definitely get agreeable with."

"Looks as if you've scored," Kinnaird told his partner.

"Aren't I the lucky one?"

"So how come Mona sent you to pick me up? She's not exactly on good terms with the law."

"She was worried about you, same as us. We think you're life's in danger. Also we'd like you to help Mona out of a jam."

"First things first, tell me about this danger with my name on it?" She asked interestedly.

"Do you recall a client that you shared with Tina Wilson called Hastings?"

"Maybe," she replied quickly, without thinking too hard. "What's so special about him?"

"We believe that he and someone else have been responsible for a number of recent deaths north of the river. Unfortunately a few innocent people have also been killed, but up until that happened Hastings and his friend specialised in attacks on toms. Hasting's partner seems to be a redhead who's useful with a knife, and likes to claw people with her nails. Apparently she almost hospitalised Tina Wilson."

"So why don't you ask Tina about them?"

"Tina's dead, Lenny too." Kinnaird watched the young woman's reaction, but news of the deaths barely registered more than a little surprise.

"Lenny didn't count," she settled back on the seat.

"He thought he did."

"How'd Tina get it?"

"Her throat was cut. Lenny and Tina's sister were thrown out of a second-floor window. We think Hastings and the redhead are getting rid of anyone who can identify them, obviously that includes you. We'd like you to identify Hastings to us."

"Is Mona involved in any of this?"

"Not as far as we know, but then anyone in your game has to be a target, especially if they're operating north of the river."

"Sounds like I got out in the nick of time."

"Maybe, unless you're going to tell us that Hastings is connected to Fisher, and that this is all about a gang war for the north's territory?"

"That would make it simple for you, wouldn't it? All you'd have to do is nick Sonny and supposedly the killings would stop."

"Are you going to tell us we're wrong, that we're simply dealing with a couple of nutters who've decided to clean up the streets?"

"I'm not going to tell you anything, at least, not until I've had a chance to speak to Mona." She crossed her legs and looked away.

"What're you doing with Fisher?"

"You want pictures?"

"An explanation. Mona seems to believe you still love her?"

"What of it?"

"So why're you with Fisher if you love someone else?" Kinnaird pushed, testing to hear if the explanation was the same as the one Mona had told them. He was also curious to discover exactly when she had known about Fisher sending the goon squad to eliminate the competition.

"Mona's been too serious lately and he's fun. There's nothing hard to understand in that."

"For you, maybe," Mowatt glanced in the rear-view mirror and caught her eye. "Why are you mixed up with Fisher when women are more your scene?"

"You're right about that, honey," she leaned forward and lay a hand on Mowatt's shoulder.

"Forget it!" Mowatt snapped, her expression frosty.

"Is she yours?" The blonde withdrew her hand.

"We're just good friends," Kinnaird said.

"For your information, sweetie, Sonny's also loaded, that's why I stay with him."

"But you must think something of Mona, otherwise you wouldn't be here?"

"Guess I must. What's your angle?"

"We're holding her temporarily, trouble is, as soon as she gets out Fisher's likely to have another go at killing her, unless we put him inside."

"And that's where I come in?"

"With him out of the way you and Mona could get back to where you were."

"I'm not into stitching up my friends," she folded her arms and sat back again.

"What about Mona?"

"Whatever they've got to sort out about me they'll have to do it without my help."

"This thing's a bit one-sided y'know. Fisher isn't playing games, he's going to kill her. If you think anything of Mona . . . . she needs your help. She was worried enough about you to send us down here."

"I don't have to do anything I don't want to do, and this I don't want to do!"

"Would it bother you if Fisher were locked up because Mona spoke against him in court?"

"Not if that's what she wants, it's her choice."

"But you won't help her?"

"Right!"

The parts of the jigsaw that Kinnaird had hoped Debbie Ash would furnish were still missing. Ash either knew very little or was being reluctant to give anything up. What her motives might be if the latter were true were not easy to decide. The same could be said about her feelings towards Sonny Fisher and Mona Curtis. She wanted Kinnaird to believe that her reason for not helping put Fisher behind bars was because he was a friend, but the detective found that hard to accept. Debbie Ash came across as totally devoid of emotion, the kind so hardened by street life her feelings had sunk to an unfathomable depth. Finally, if she knew Hastings and the redhead, what could she gain by keeping their identities secret? It dawned on him that she might be putting up a front by acting casual, when in reality she was scared, as Jones had been.

"Are you going to talk to us about Hastings or the redhead?"

"I'm thinking it over. How much would you be willing to pay for the information?"

"Isn't saving your life enough?"

"I'm not certain that I'm in danger, you're the ones saying that I am."

"If you've anything worth hearing I can stretch to fifteen quid."

"That's not very persuasive considering I could be handing you a couple of murderers on a plate."

He had an urge to grab her by the throat and shake the

information out of her, but decided against it. She might have enjoyed it too much. "OK, maybe we can go a little higher, but I want to be certain that the people you tell us about are the ones that you passed to Tina Wilson. I don't want anything duff, otherwise I promise you'll be sorry."

"I knew someone called Hastings, and I did pass him to Tina. She was always hungry for bread, that pimp cost her plenty."

"What about the redhead, did he ever bring a woman with him?"

"No, more's the pity, it might've been fun."

"What else can you tell us about him? Do you have his address, a telephone number, his real name? Did he hurt you?"

"He got off on hurting people." She paused, leaned back on the seat and glanced out of a side window. "Look, I'm a working girl. I've already given you enough without getting anything in return, so how much is his address worth?"

"Tina's dead," Kinnaird pleaded. "So is her kid sister and Sheenarena, plus a few others. We think your life is on the line, so why don't you just tell us what you know?"

"They're lucky, they've escaped this shitty world, but I still have to live here. Now how much?"

He pulled out his wallet and flicked through a small wad of five pound notes. It occurred to him that she was probably carrying a hundred times more in the money pouch around her waist. When he offered her twenty pounds she leaned forward and plucked more out of his wallet.

"Thanks for leaving me something." He stared at a lonely five pound note she had left him, thinking Curtis had been right about her greed.

"You're getting this on the cheap. Christ, I trick for double what's here!"

He resisted a verbal speculation about some people's idea of value for money, "So what have you got?"

"I'll give you his address, after I've seen Mona."

Kinnaird grabbed her lapels and pulled her up close, "Do you think this is a game?"

"I'm not that dumb, but I want to see Mona, and I don't trust you enough to believe that once you've got what you want, you'll let me do that!"

He glanced at Mowatt, but she simply shrugged her shoulders. "OK, Debbie. You can see Mona, but you won't be leaving the station until you've given us that address."

She prised his hands free of her lapels and sat back on the seat. "No problem."

Debbie Ash spent an hour with Mona Curtis. When she emerged from the cell she gave Kinnaird what she had agreed, an address for Hastings which turned out to be in Kensington. "How'd it go with Mona?"

"Fine, she needed to see me. I think she understands how things are now. What's going to happen to her over this morning's shooting? She's worried sick."

"She shouldn't be, it was self-defence."

"I talked to her about going to court over it, and she isn't keen on testifying against Sonny Fisher."

"She doesn't have a choice if she wants that contract lifted."

"I think I can help out. She wants me to try, and I said I would. She'd rather take her chances with me than the law."

Kinnaird suddenly understood why Debbie Ash had wanted to talk to Curtis. She was looking after her own interests. With Sonny Fisher in prison his empire would be open to a takeover, and it was doubtful Ash would be welcome. On top of that she had fallen out with Duffy, and was unable to return north of the Thames. In a very short time she could easily be a young woman with nowhere to go. Kinnaird glanced at the address she had given him, "Do you know if Hastings is involved with Fisher?"

"I don't think so, he's just a perv. Sorry if that ruins your ideas about a takeover, but that's how it is."

"What will you tell Fisher when you go back?" It troubled Kinnaird that Debbie Ash refuted the notion of a gang takeover; as far as he was concerned, all the signs pointed to it. Yet she wasn't alone, the inspector and the chief inspector both held great store by the idea that a couple of crazies were responsible for the attacks on the prostitute population.

"That Duffy sent his people after me, and that I managed to give them the slip."

"That might start off something big."

"You should worry, you'll only have to pick up the pieces when it's over." She patted the money pouch around her waist, "Thanks for the dosh. I hope you get him, I'll be watching the headlines to see if you do."

As she walked away from the police station Mowatt joined Kinnaird at the main entrance. "Confident cow isn't she?"

"You didn't like her?"

"Call it female intuition, but she gave me a bad feeling, like she's laughing at us."

"We'll see her again if she is, but your intuition might be responding to the clumsy pass she made at you."

"That's got nothing to do with it!"

"Sure. Go call Kensington's collator and check out the name and address she's given us, and don't forget to tell the station officer we'll be on his ground in less than an hour. I'm going to talk to Colin Evans."

Kinnaird found the DI alone in his office and explained what Ash had given them. Evans wasn't the type to impress easily, but he did look a little relieved that someone had at last found a promising lead.

"Have you checked the address with Kensington yet?"

"Mel's doing that now," Kinnaird replied, his own excitement growing. Things were suddenly moving, an arrest was imminent and with luck he would be the one to make it. Bonner would be avenged.

"Well if there's nothing on it you'd better get round there pronto, we don't wanting him slipping away." The DI began to show signs of urgency, but for different reasons. Detective Chief Inspector Ship had been making a nuisance of himself, pestering Evans hourly for an update on how the investigation was proceeding, and the DI was tired of having to give him the same negative answer.

"I'd like us to be tooled up, just in case."

Evans nodded without argument, unusual for him, guns being another of his dislikes. "I suppose it's justified under the circumstances." He rose from the chair and moved to the front of the desk. "I should really be going with you, but I've plenty to keep me occupied here."

"I can take care of it."

The DI stared out through the glass partition that separated his office from the rest of the CID. "You should have a DS in charge at the very least, but wouldn't you believe it there isn't one out there."

"It's still only an enquiry, Colin."

"Yeah, but an armed one. Take a few blokes with you,

110

and make sure none of them shoots an innocent bystander, that kind of headache I can do without!"

Mowatt came into the office, her face flushed as she too felt the growing sense of excitement created by Debbie Ash. "Nothing's known about who lives at the address."

The DI nodded, "Get going!"

The night crept across the sky covering the city with a blanket of darkness as the detectives arrived at the Kensington address. It was a four-storey Georgian house located in a mews with a narrow alley running down one side towards an adjoining thoroughfare. A couple of street lamps threw a gentle glow against the building, turning its white paint yellow. Inside lights downstairs shone behind a thin veil of curtains.

Four other officers accompanied Kinnaird and Mowatt, all experienced detective constables, armed with Smith and Wesson .38 revolvers. Only Mowatt was unarmed, but she still insisted on remaining by Kinnaird's side as they approached the front door. A couple of detectives, Ben Keyes and Gordon Matthews, scurried around back to cover the garden, while another pair, Chris Mullins and Andy Paige, listened to Kinnaird try one last time to persuade Mowatt to get behind them.

"I deserve to be beside you!" she insisted without making any move to drop back.

"You might get hurt!"

"So might you!"

"I've a gun, you haven't. There's no argument."

"If anything goes wrong, you don't have to worry, I won't ask for your help, Kinnaird!"

Behind them Mullins decided he had heard enough. "Christ,

Del, let her stay beside you if she's so keen to be a target."

"Thanks for the support, Mullins!" she snapped over her shoulder.

"It's too late anyway," Paige said as they stopped at the front door.

Kinnaird used a bell and tried to ignore her. From behind the door a man's voice asked a question. "Who is it, what do you want?"

"It's the police, we'd like to talk to a Mr Hastings."

"There's no one by that name here." A spy hole in the door showed signs of movement. "I don't know you, what police station are you from?"

"Fulham. Can we talk to you face to face, I'm not in the habit of carrying out discussions through doors?"

It struck Kinnaird as odd that the man might recognise local officers, particularly as Mowatt had been given no information relating to the address from Kensington's collator or station officer. Yet he was too concerned about the man's reluctance to open the door to dwell on its significance.

A moment later the door opened on a chain. "I want to see some identification."

Kinnaird showed the man his warrant card, "We're investigating a murder, and were told the man we want to interview, named Hastings, lives here."

"And I'm telling you no one by that names lives here. So I can't help you." He studied them through the narrow gap; he was a tall man, at least four inches taller than Kinnaird.

"What's your name?" the detective asked.

"Macaulay. Who's been murdered?"

"Several prostitutes." Macaulay glared at them through the narrow gap, his voice choked with apprehension, "Who

112

d'you really work for, you're not police. Is it Fisher?"

"Open the door, Mr Macaulay!" Kinnaird ordered, unwilling to accept further delay.

"No way, get out of here!" Macaulay tried to slam the door shut, but Kinnaird blocked him. Then Mullins and Paige crowded over Mowatt and combined their strength to force the door open.

"Let's kick it in, Del!" Paige shouted.

"If you're really police there'll be trouble over this!" Macaulay yelled, as their combined weight quickly overwhelmed him and the door chain. They burst into a hall, but he had a head start, racing upstairs as the detectives stumbled. As he ran Macaulay shouted at the top of his voice, "Katie, call the police!"

That it was an odd thing for him to do registered with Kinnaird, but there was no time to think, only act. As Macaulay disappeared into a room at the end of a landing, its door closing behind him, the detectives raced towards it. Downstairs a woman suddenly rushed across the hall, and Kinnaird watched as she stopped at the entrance shrieking at the top of her voice.

"Go grab her, Mel." Kinnaird stopped the other detectives on the landing, and gave himself time to think. He could not understand Macaulay's reaction or that of the woman. The detectives watched Mowatt attempt to calm her, using soothing words in an effort to stop her screaming. Only after she had produced her warrant card did the woman fall silent, taking time to study the words written on Mowatt's ID.

"There's no place to hide, Macaulay, we've got the back of the house covered. Come out so that we can get this thing sorted." A volley of shots ripped through the door, peppering Kinnaird with splinters of wood. He and the others hit the floor face down, quickly pulling out their own hardware and blasting off the lock. The door swung silently inwards exposing a darkened room with a moonlit window for a backdrop. "Give it up, Macaulay, there's no need for this!"

"You've come to kill me, but I won't die alone!" Another couple of shots burst from the darkened room, thudding into a wall close to where the detectives lay.

"This bloke's a raving loony," Paige muttered.

"No one's going to shoot you, Macaulay, not if you throw out your weapon!"

"John, John, they really are the police, don't shoot!" The woman suddenly rushed up from downstairs and ran along the landing towards where Macaulay was hiding. Kinnaird grabbed her, held her, but she fought him, not wanting to be stopped. Macaulay fired wildly, and bullets flew dangerously close over their heads. "John . . . . John it's me, Katie. Listen, they really are the police, there's been a mix up. It's all a mistake!"

Kinnaird dropped to his knees and took Katie down on the floor with him, "Who the hell does he think we are?"

"Sonny Fisher's men," she stared at him as if he should have known. "Where've you been living, Mars? Don't you know there's a gang war on?"

Kinnaird dragged her against a wall out of the line of fire, "And what does Macaulay have to do with it?"

"My husband is Martin Duffy's accountant, damn you. Now do you understand? We've had all kinds of threats, he's been living on his nerves waiting for Fisher to strike for the past month!"

Suddenly what Kinnaird had suspected all along acquired credibility, because who and what Macaulay represented immediately became crystal clear. He was Duffy's right-hand man, known to the police only as 'the accountant', someone never properly identified, because that had been the way Duffy had kept it. Macaulay operated behind the scenes, living off the spoils from a vice empire simply by keeping the vice king's books in order for the Inland Revenue. Now war had been declared with only the factions involved aware. The attacks on the prostitutes north of the Thames were part of that war, yet Debbie Ash had sent Kinnaird to Macaulay, a man with supposedly more to lose than gain by attacking the women his partner employed. He studied the woman he held, a striking blonde in her mid-thirties who would never have been found playing the role of a prostitute. Was it just feasible that was part of the reason for her husband to enjoy a sadistic perversion outside of their home? Macaulay fitted the description they had for Hastings, he was also privy to intimate knowledge of the girls working for Duffy, and there was every chance some would have known him. Sheenarena for one. If his sadism were out of control, Kinnaird could understand why he would want to keep it hidden from Duffy. Yet it was not enough of a reason for Macaulay to fear any serious retribution if the vice king discovered his perverted idiosyncrasy. Duffy had priorities, like any businessman, and maintaining presentable accounts for the Inland Revenue was probably at the top. The detective did not doubt that Macaulay was a prized partner. Someone who could get away with almost anything, including murder, provided Duffy's accounts were properly maintained. Yet Macaulay was frightened, and obviously expecting an attack from someone. Sonny Fisher was the most likely candidate, and that the detective found confusing. If Fisher were waging a vice war striking at Duffy's prostitutes, beating, killing, and ultimately intimidating them off the streets in order to put the vice king out of business, Debbie Ash's accusation that Macaulay was a sadistic killer became lost in the overall scenario. He couldn't be working for Sonny Fisher, yet if he were the killer the police were hunting, he was also ruining Duffy's business, and Fisher would have no reason to want him dead, quite the opposite.

"We need to talk to him," he heard himself say to the woman. "Do you think you can get him to throw out the gun?"

"Promise me that you won't kill him. He's all I've got, and I don't want to lose him, no matter what anyone thinks of him."

"If he puts his gun down there won't be a need for any of us to get hurt. Convince him of that and I promise he won't be harmed."

"Why do you need to talk to him?"

"A young woman alleged that he's responsible for attacks on prostitutes working for Duffy."

"That's madness, why should someone say such a thing?"

"The fact is someone did, and we need to talk to him about it."

"I'll get him to come out. Give me a few minutes." She began to rise to her feet but the detective held her. "He'll need to be convinced that you won't shoot him. I have to stand in the doorway when I talk to him."

"I'll stand with you."

"But you could get shot."

"I'm gambling he'll know a hired gun wouldn't offer himself as a target." He came off the floor and together they moved into the open doorway.

"John, it's me, Katie, can you see me?"

"What're you doing, Katie? Has he forced you to come to the door?"

116

"John, I'm detective constable Kinnaird from Fulham. We don't want to hurt you. We were told you were responsible for the murders I mentioned. We weren't taking chances and came here in force, but it looks as if there's been a mistake. Please come out so we can clear this up."

There was a moment's silence before Macaulay replied, "But why would anyone say such a thing?"

"Someone has, Mr Macaulay, and we had to respond," Kinnaird said. "Please come out."

A shape moved cautiously towards them, the gun obvious in his hand as he passed the bedroom window. Then Kinnaird spotted the tell-tale sign of movement outside as someone blocked out the moonlight, and a chill raced down his spine. "Macaulay get down!"

His words were lost in an the explosion that shattered a windowpane into a million pieces. Macaulay looked as if someone punched him in the back before dropping forward on to his face. Kinnaird quickly rushed to his side, kneeled down and heard him gasp. The bedroom lights came on as the detective shouted for an ambulance. Macaulay's wife stood over them, her face horrified by the sight of blood spreading over the back of her husband's white shirt. Her legs buckled and she dropped to her knees alongside him. She wept, her head shaking, not wanting to believe what her eyes were telling her. Mowatt ran into the bedroom with a towel and covered Macaulay's wound, glancing at Kinnaird who slowly rose to his feet as Mullins opened the smashed window for the officers outside. Detective Constable Mike Keyes climbed into the bedroom, a smoking gun still in his hand.

"You OK, Del?" Keyes glanced down at Macaulay.

"I saw he had the drop on you. I thought you were a gonna, when he moved I let him have it." Kinnaird nodded, unable to find the words to say it was a mistake. "We saw the gun flashes from the garden and climbed up a ladder."

"He was coming out!" Mrs Macaulay said in a hushed voice that silenced him. "You shot him for nothing!"

"The murders of more than half-a-dozen people are hardly nothing!" Keyes replied.

"My husband didn't kill them! You shot the wrong bloody man, you idiot!"

"He didn't know," Kinnaird told her and touched her shoulder, but she shrugged him off.

"Don't you dare touch me, you said he wouldn't be hurt if I got him to come out, it's as much your fault as anyone's!" Tears ran freely down her face as she looked around at the other detectives surrounding them. Anger, fear and despair were all neatly wrapped up in her expression as she rose to her feet. "You're all to blame, excuses won't save any of you. If he dies I'll see justice done if it's the last thing I ever do, and that's a promise!"

"Is it true, Del?" Keyes holstered his gun, his expression grave, his gaze fixed on the man he had shot.

The detective was in his early thirties with eight years service, two commendations for valour and an above average crime arrest record. On top of that he was a member of the F division firearms team, and regularly won trophies for his shooting prowess. Yet suddenly none of that mattered, blown away in the split second he had pulled a trigger.

"Maybe, Mike, we can't be certain. He works for Duffy, and allegedly started shooting because he thought we were sent by the opposition to waste him."

"And you've done them a big favour, haven't you?" Mrs Macaulay glared at Keyes, her small fists clenched tightly at her sides. "Get out of my house!"

Kinnaird nodded. The other detective hesitated as if he wanted to say something to her, then turned away and walked out of the bedroom.

"I'm going to need a fresh towel, Del. Will you keep this one on him while I go find another . . . . Perhaps you can help me, Mrs Macaulay?" Mowatt stared up at them, her intuition telling her to get the woman out of sight of her husband. There was too much blood, too much mess, and not enough hope in her eyes.

"He's going to die," Mrs Macaulay sighed grimly staring down at them as Kinnaird changed places with Mowatt. The female detective put an arm around her shoulders and gently led her out of the bedroom. At about the same time the thunder of feet racing up the stairs outside announced the arrival of medical aid. An ambulance crew appeared at the bedroom door and quickly took charge of Macaulay. Within a few minutes he was being carried out on a stretcher, followed closely by his wife. Kinnaird asked Mowatt to go with her, but she held back.

"I forgot to do a couple of things that I think were important." He studied her, seeing some of the blame for what had happened in her eyes. "I didn't warn Kensington's station officer that we'd be on his ground, and I didn't ask for a check in the voters' register when I spoke to a PC covering for the collator."

"No one knew Macaulay was Duffy's number two, except maybe Debbie Ash, and she didn't warn us. If this is anybody's fault, then it's hers. Don't get excited about not telling the station officer about us, it isn't worth it. Now you'd better go with the Macaulays." Kinnaird remained in the bedroom after she had gone, staring down at the blood-stained carpet while he sat on a bed.

"This turned into a bloody mess," Paige said from the door. "Mike Keyes is having a fit of depression, and Evans is hopping mad. He's on his way over."

"I don't blame either of them," Kinnaird replied without looking up.

A couple of CID officers from Kensington were with Kinnaird in the bedroom when Evans arrived. The DI came in, asked them to leave, closed the door and pulled up a chair as Kinnaird sat down on the bed. "I want to hear this in detail."

He covered all the events leading up to Macaulay's shooting, only omitting that Mowatt had not warned Kensington's station officer of their presence in the local area. "I want to bring in Debbie Ash and find out why she pointed us in Macaulay's direction."

"Before you do any more flying around there's something else you should know . . . . "

Kinnaird beat him to it. "That the CID at Kensington suspected Macaulay of working for Duffy?" Evans nodded. "Their blokes were just telling me."

"Your partner, Mowatt, fouled up. She was meant to check. If she had, things might've worked out differently."

"There's no point looking at her for a scapegoat, Colin, I was in charge of this. I should have checked that she'd done it. She told me that she forgot."

"In this game no one's allowed the luxury of a poor memory, especially when something like this happens!"

"It's my responsibility."

The DI showed little anger. Perhaps he had spent it up on the way to the house, but his tone was no less menacing. "Then they'll cane you for it, if Macaulay isn't our killer."

Kinnaird knew that he was right, guessed that Evans had

been thinking through a worst-case scenario on the journey to Kensington. He too would take a share of the blame; no one involved, however indirectly, would come through unscathed. Yet that only angered Kinnaird, "How? By sending me back on the beat? Maybe I could use the exercise?"

"Talk like that again and I'll personally see it happens!" He pushed up from the chair and moved around the blood stained carpet. "I've a share in the blame. I should have put a DS in charge or come with you myself."

"It wouldn't have changed anything. Macaulay fitted the description we had for Hastings and started shooting at us. On top of that we still don't know for certain that he isn't the killer." Even as Kinnaird said it, he sensed Macaulay would prove to be innocent.

"But you know it's what they're going to say. Another bloke might've handled the initial contact differently. At least a DS would've had the rank to collect flak."

"I don't care about being their scapegoat."

"I'll remind you of that the first time I hear you moan when you're back in uniform. Where's Keyes?"

"Downstairs with Chris Mullins expecting to be charged with manslaughter."

"First Macaulay has to die, but from what you've told me I can't see that Keyes had any choice. Mike's not trigger-happy, he thought he was saving your life, and that's the way I'm going to argue it. I'd have been less happy if you'd been the one shot!"

"Mrs Macaulay wouldn't agree with you."

"Get Keyes to come up and see me, then go collect your partner from the hospital. There's nothing more you can do here except get under my feet!"

Kinnaird found his partner sitting with Mrs Macaulay outside an operating theatre. The detective avoided being seen by the woman Mowatt was comforting, keeping to an adjacent corridor until she looked in his direction, then waved at her to join him. "How is she?"

"Calmer now, but she's frightened for him, it's natural. He's been in there for over an hour."

"You look tired, do you want me to get someone else to sit with her?"

"Not yet, I think she's taken to me. It might not be the same with someone else."

"OK, well I'll be around to take you home when you're ready. I'm going to see Greg. He'll give me hell if he ever found out that I was here and didn't pay him a visit."

"Did you see Evans?" She sensed trouble from the look he gave her, and was suddenly concerned, the blame for what had happened re-emerging in her eyes. "My not telling Kensington we were going to Macaulay's address is a problem isn't it?"

"Nothing too terrible. Apparently the CID had begun to suspect Macaulay of being in league with Duffy, the station officer would have known that. But don't worry, I was in charge, it was my responsibility to ensure that you did all that was required."

"I don't need you to get me off the hook, Del!" She rounded on him so forcibly he stepped back in surprise. "I'm the one who forgot, it's my fault!"

"I'm not trying to get you off the hook, Mel. I'm simply telling you how it is. I was in charge because I was the senior officer, and you're meant to be learning from me. If you do something wrong it's because I didn't push hard enough for you to do it, right?"

Mowatt fell silent, uncertain about her own position because of the strength of his retort. Yet she wasn't about to let it end there, "Did you tell him that Macaulay could have shot you, that you offered yourself as a target?"

"I was making a bid to save a disaster from happening. In the end it was a futile gesture, but I'm glad you noticed. You're actually starting to sound as if you like me."

"Just your nerve, Kinnaird. It starts and ends there!"

"If I wasn't happily attached, and we weren't forced to work together, I'd have said that was a pity."

"I guess that I should be thankful about something after all. I never could get used to the sight of seeing a grown man cry when I turn him down."

"Keep punching, Mowatt," he laughed and turned away. "I'll be back to collect you in an hour."

Kinnaird found Wright lying on his side reading his favourite newspaper – the *Sporting Life*. Wright was a inveterate gambler who had often come close to bankruptcy, and been on the receiving end of unfair criticism from colleagues because of it. Yet, somehow, Lady Luck always sprang up just in the nick of time to save him from the brink of disaster, pushing the fateful day when things would finally never work out further into an inevitable future. In many ways, and gambling was one, he and Kinnaird were so dissimilar people wondered what it was that kept their relationship alive. Sometimes Kinnaird did the same. Wright's face brightened as his friend stepped through the door. "Good to see you, pal."

"You should be asleep."

Wright groaned, "I sleep all day as well as night. I might as well be dead for all the action I get. I really could use some fresh air."

"I don't know of any bookies who have that on offer, none that I've followed you into anyway."

"What they offer is a good substitute."

Kinnaird pulled up a chair and sat down, "When are you meant to be getting out?"

"In about two weeks after Christmas is over and we're into next year! Even then I won't be able to go straight back to work. I'm told that I should take a couple of weeks off convalescing, and Karen won't have it any other way either!"

"Well I'm missing you partner."

"It's mutual, have they fixed you up with anyone else?"

"A plonk, probationer off the Crime Squad called Mowatt."

"But you don't work with women, everyone knows that." Wright made it sound as if there had been a mistake. "Didn't you argue?"

"I argued."

"So what happened?"

"Melanie Mowatt is my partner."

Wright shook his head sympathetically, "What does she look like?"

"Pretty, thirty-eight, twenty-four, thirty-six."

"I hope that's an educated guess, I wouldn't want to think my being put in here has done anything to damage your relationship with Vienna." Wright had initially been doubtful about Kinnaird's friendship with the young woman. Then during the past year Wright noticed a change in his friend, a subtle softening, as a more relaxed and happier person began to emerge.

"No chance, even though Mel is a looker."

"Glad to hear it. So how's our investigation proceeding? Have you got anyone for sticking a blade in my back?"

"Things aren't going well. No, that's an understatement,

things are a shambles." Kinnaird then repeated all the events that had occurred since Wright had been in hospital, and somehow the sharing of it seemed to lessen his load. A little over an hour later he stepped out of Wright's room with more ideas and a little extra strength to face what lay ahead. Also, he had relearned one of the reasons why their relationship survived.

He found Mowatt asleep on a bench in casualty, and gently shook her awake. She stirred like a cat, uncurled and stretched her arms above her head before rising to her feet. "What time is it?"

"Late. What happened to Macaulay?"

"They took the bullet out, but it'll be another twenty-four hours before they know if he's going to survive for certain. Mrs Macaulay was given a spare room for the night. How's Greg?"

"He'll be out in about ten days."

"Did you tell him about me?"

"Sure."

"What did you say?" She shook her head, "No don't tell me, I know it had to be disgusting."

"OK, I won't tell you," he shrugged, unconcerned as they moved towards the exit. Outside the night was cold, a layer of icy moisture covering his car.

"So what did you tell him about me?" Mowatt asked, unable to control her curiosity.

He unlocked the car door, "I thought you didn't want to know?"

"I changed my mind."

"I said that you were good in a tight corner."

A wealth of surprise lit up her face, "Did you really?"

"I'm not going to lie to you about it, Mel. That's what I told him."

"What else?"

"Christ, woman, what is this? You want to hear everything that was said in a private conversation?"

"Just the bits about me. Does he think that I've been overwhelmed by your irresistible charm?"

"My ego doesn't require that kind of boost. I told him that we weren't playing around, and he was glad. He likes Vienna, thinks that she's done me the world of good." He climbed into the car and reached across to release her door.

Mowatt settled down beside him, "Thanks for not telling him anything about me which isn't true."

"You were anticipating something different?"

"Some blokes like to tell their friends they're shagging the life out of me. That I'm a nymphomaniac who's so man-hungry, I can't wait till I get them alone. It's all macho bullshit, but you'd be surprised how many times it's happened . . . . I thought you might be the same. I guess I was wrong."

"I guess you were." He started the engine and drove them out of the hospital carpark headed towards the police section house at Ravenscourt Park where Mowatt had accommodation.

"Del, I don't think Macaulay's our man. I spoke to his wife in some depth and it just doesn't gel. He might be big but I didn't get the impression that there's an aggressive streak in him, he comes across as too nervy for anything like that. He's been scared witless by what's been happening between Fisher and Duffy, that's why he had the gun. As for beating up prostitutes, we're talking about a man who won't even stamp on spiders. This is one big gentle man, that's what she made me believe."

"But then she would, wouldn't she?"

"Perhaps, but I think she told me the truth. There was no point her lying with him banging at death's door."

"I hear what you're saying, Mel, but if he's a pervert he could be hiding it from her; it's been done before."

"It wouldn't go down too well if he turned out not to be our man would it, Del?"

"What're you getting at?" He frowned as the mood between them suddenly changed.

"An innocent man being shot by police is going to cause everyone involved in a lot of flak. I suppose it's better to think Macaulay's guilty, isn't it?"

"I don't like what I'm hearing you say, Mowatt. I'm not in the business of stitching innocent people up, but Macaulay fits Hastings' description, and he would know where to attack Duffy's women. On top of that Debbie Ash sent us to him."

"That's right, Debbie Ash did, didn't she? And she's now back with Fisher."

"What's that supposed to mean?"

"I don't know. Of the two I believe Mrs Macaulay."

Kinnaird drove on in silence, thinking about Debbie Ash, and trying to provide her with a motive for sending them to Macaulay's address. The trouble was that the motive was obvious, the one Mowatt had provided. Ash did work for Fisher, and getting Macaulay out of the way weakened Duffy, but using the police to do it was clever. He was still thinking about it as he pulled up outside the section house. Mowatt thanked him for the ride, climbed out of the car and headed towards the entrance without saying another word.

When he arrived home Vienna was awake in bed, naked beneath a robe as she read one of her college books. Her arms slipped around his neck as he kneeled on the floor beside her, "You look like you've had a tough day?"

"It's been full of problems, how about you?"

"I doubt it was as harrowing as yours, I managed to struggle against a sea of shoppers and bought a few more Christmas presents. That was probably the highlight of my day." She was staring deeply into his dark eyes, seeing things no one else had ever seen. "How's your new partner working out?"

"She's doing all right."

"You haven't said much about her. Is she pretty?"

"Do you think I'd notice when I've got you?"

Her hands clamped on his ears in a tight embrace while her eyes narrowed suspiciously, "Yes, so is she?"

"Ow! She's all right."

"You bastard!"

"Hey, that hurts!" he winced as she tugged on his ears. "What did you do that for?"

"She must be damn beautiful, that's why!" She released him, her face creasing with mock anger. "Whenever a man says that a woman looks all right, it means he thinks she's as horny as hell!"

"You know better than that." He rose to his feet, shrugged his coat and jacket off his shoulders, kicked off his shoes, then climbed on to the bed. Vienna watched as he straddled her, his knees either side of her slim waist. "I've found my soulmate."

"I like to hear you say it." Her back came off the pillow as he slipped the robe from her shoulders and cupped her bare breasts.

"Do you want to talk about what's made you look like you've been through a war?"

He climbed off the bed and removed the remainder of his clothes, then slipped beneath the duvet. She wrapped herself around him, her soft curves pillowing his tension, willing his muscles to relax. Slowly he began to talk about his day, and she listened, never interrupting, letting her body help caress away his anxieties. When he had finished they made love, explosively, the final therapy to help him see events in perspective. She would always be there, no matter what happened in the world outside, and knowing that helped him more than anything he had ever known.

FIVE

When Kinnaird arrived at the station next morning, Colin Evans was in his office with Detective Chief Inspector George Ship. Evans had been up for most of the night, and it showed. By contrast the DCI looked as if he were attempting to set new standards in immaculate personal presentation. Kinnaird joined Clements, and pretended to study the chessboard beside his desk.

"They've been like that for fifteen minutes," Clements told him without looking up. "It's you they're discussing. Have you seen the papers this morning?" He pulled a tabloid out of a desk drawer without waiting for Kinnaird to reply. "Front page is an eye-catcher."

The headline lacked imagination, but the clerk had been right, it did catch the eye. Alongside a brief article reporting that *Starsky and Hutch* was the most popular detective series on TV, was another about Macaulay. It read: "POLICE GUN DOWN INNOCENT MAN". There was nothing about Macaulay still being the chief suspect to half-a-dozen murders. Whoever had leaked news of the shooting had offered a very limited viewpoint, ensuring the police took a hammering. Kinnaird wondered if that's what it took to sell papers.

"They even spelled your name right," Clements pointed to a part where Kinnaird was mentioned as the officer leading an assault team.

"I was born for stardom."

"I think the flak's about to fly. Evans is waving for you to join them."

The detective headed towards the DI's office with the clerk wishing him luck. Colin Evans sat behind his desk puffing on a fat cigar while DCI Ship stared out of a window overlooking the station yard. Kinnaird closed the door and stood in front of the DI's desk.

Ship sighed, and did the talking without turning away from the window, "I want a statement from you about last night's shooting. Make certain you omit nothing."

"Yes, sir." A lull in their brief conversation made Kinnaird think that was all the DCI had to say, but Ship cleared his throat and begun again.

"From what the DI tells me you may have acted a little hastily last night." Kinnaird glanced at Evans, but the DI was stony-faced, impossible to read. Ship continued, "Apparently you also neglected to inform anyone at Kensington that you were going to be on their patch. You might have saved us from a great deal of criticism if you had performed that basic piece of police practice." Kinnaird remained silent as the Chief Inspector turned away from the window and faced him. "Of course, in the situation confronting you last night a more senior officer should have been present, but then, that was not your fault."

There it was, the first indication that Evans had received a reprimand, but the DI was not about to argue with the DCI in front of one of his men. Kinnaird had other ideas. "I don't agree. I'm as experienced as any DS in this office. The shooting had nothing to do with rank or the way I approached the situation."

The DCI had been in the Force for twenty years. He was

in his mid-fifties though a full head of dark hair helped disguise his age. His reddish purple complexion suggested either high blood pressure or heavy drinking. The latter was not his style. "An innocent man shot in his home suggests that you're wrong, Kinnaird."

"Who says he's innocent? I thought that still had to be proved."

"It's been proved, beyond doubt!" Ship came away from the window and stood in front of the detective with just a couple of inches separating them. "Mrs Macaulay has been able to furnish us with alibis for her husband's movements on every occasion an attack took place. The man's innocent, Kinnaird, and you're partly responsible for his being shot!"

"Macaulay's responsible for getting himself shot. Keyes reacted to the gun flashes he spotted from the garden and thought he was saving my life."

Ship silenced him with a wave of his hand, "I've heard it all, but it might not have gone that far if you'd controlled the situation at the front door. If he dies . . . . "

Kinnaird's career hinged on Macaulay's survival, the detective had guessed as much, but not until now had anyone actually voiced the fact. A sacrifice would be made in the event of the accountant's death, and Kinnaird was it. His initial approach was where they would pin the blame, no matter what anyone else said in his defence. He saw Evans frown as if to deter him from speaking again, but he wanted to hear Ship spell it out. "If Macaulay lives I may get another chance, is that what you're saying?"

"The final decision won't be mine," the DCI replied so coolly the words almost froze on the tip of his tongue. "If there's evidence for a case to be brought against you then, rest assured, it will happen."

"Am I suspended?"

"Not for now." Ship made it sound inevitable.

"What about Keyes?"

"You've yourself to worry about, Kinnaird, but consider yourself lucky that it wasn't you who actually pulled the trigger. Keyes will be suspended pending a full enquiry." The DCI glanced at Evans then back to him,

"That's all."

He stepped out of the DI's office and waited with Clements until Ship had gone, then returned to Evans for a final say. "I know just how you're feeling, Del, but he does have a lot to contend with. It isn't going to be easy salvaging our credibility after last night."

"Don't expect my sympathy, we both know that nothing could have altered what happened last night. Macaulay was shooting at us, damn it!"

"You can't say that events leading up to the shooting might not have been different with someone else taking the lead. After all, there aren't too many people who'd have offered themselves as a target to prise a bloke out of hiding. Ironically your bravery is what got us into this mess but, as yet, possessing courage isn't a crime. Also looked at in the cold light of day your misdemeanours don't amount to much, yet they'll make it appear as if they do, should Macaulay not survive."

"What about you? It looked to me as if you've been given a going over."

"In the end I'm a survivor, same as you, and Keyes."

Evans blew out a thick cloud of cigar smoke that lingered over his head. "Now, what are we going to do about catching these killers?"

"Debbie Ash is the one who got us into this mess. I'll have

another go at Mona Curtis to see if she'll tell me where we can find her, because I doubt that she'll return to Brixton Market."

"But is that tom really likely to tell you anything second time around?"

"Colin, we know one thing for certain since last night. There's a gang war on, we're not simply dealing with a couple of nutters. There's also a chance Mona knows a lot more than she was willing to tell us, and this time around I think I know how I can persuade her to talk."

"Are you really certain Debbie Ash is worth the effort? I know she made you mad for steering you wrong over Macaulay, but I want the killings to stop!"

"Debbie Ash is the key, I'm certain of it."

"How're you getting on with Mowatt?" The DI slipped in a change of subject so unexpectedly that it took Kinnaird by surprise.

"She guessed Macaulay was innocent, we argued over it last night. She's got a good head on her, but I'd still sooner work with a bloke or even solo."

"You can't do either, Ship wants her with you. He thinks that she acts as an inhibitor to your impulsiveness, even after last night's episode." Kinnaird shook his head. "What you've got to understand is that the DCI wanted you taken off the investigation. I insisted you remain, but he demanded that Mowatt stay by your side. Now you'd better write up your statement covering last night. Let Mowatt try her hand at interrogating Curtis."

"I'd rather do it myself. Can't the statement wait?"

"Not even a minute longer. Come on, give Mowatt a chance to improve her interrogation technique, after all she was right about Macaulay. A fiver says she'll get what you're after."

"You're on." Kinnaird stepped out of the DI's office and wandered over to where his partner was waiting. He briefed her on what had to be done, and inwardly smiled at her surprise and delight that he was giving her a chance to interrogate Mona Curtis alone.

A couple of hours later he finished writing his statement, and felt satisfied that even the DCI would be unable to find fault with it. He hadn't seen Mowatt since she had gone downstairs to interrogate Curtis, and guessed that she was having a tougher time than either she or the DI had imagined. He took his statement to Evans. The DI ran a quick eye over it then dropped it in an out tray. "I just heard from the hospital. Macaulay's condition has stabilised. He's on the mend."

"At last some good news. Do you want me to find out how Mel's doing? It's been a couple of hours."

"Get yourself a drink, give her another fifteen minutes. Remember, I've a fiver riding on her, so don't spend all of your money in the canteen."

Mowatt joined him in the canteen a few minutes after he sat down at a table. "Mona isn't talking."

"Have you told Evans?"

"No. Do you think he's going to be disappointed?"

"I'd bet money on it." She mistook his grin for derision, and sank cheerlessly back on the chair. "Can you do better?"

"When I've finished my coffee. Wait here, I need to talk to Mona alone."

"That's against the rules, Kinnaird. Male officers require company when interrogating female prisoners. What if she screams rape? Aren't you in enough trouble?"

"It's the only way we're ever going to find Debbie Ash. The risk's worth it, especially as Macaulay is on the mend."

"He is!" She leaned forward with a look of relief that brushed away the cheerlessness.

"I want you to write your statement about last night while I'm talking to Mona. Take a look at a copy of mine. I left it on my desk." He rose from the chair and headed out of the canteen, missing the look of concern that followed him as he left her.

Mona Curtis lay stretched out on a bench with knees raised and short skirt rucked up high across her long, dark thighs, an invitation for attention that she didn't attempt to disguise as Kinnaird entered the cell.

"I'm told you're unwilling to co-operate in helping us find Debbie."

"You think that you're gonna do better than that woman officer?" She had just beaten a young probationer at interrogation, and pumped up her self-confidence to a point that assumed she could do it again, any time.

"Did Debbie tell you about Macaulay, and that you shouldn't say anything to us once she'd gone?"

"I'll be out of here soon, because you spoke up for me," she mocked him with forced laughter. "That was really good of you, but there's nothing you can do to stop me leaving, not without making things awkward for yourself. From where I'm sitting, I'd say that you've nothing more to trade for what else I know."

He sat down beside her on the bench, ignoring the leggy display. "You and Debbie had a laugh at our expense didn't you? She wanted Duffy weakened because she works for Fisher, and us taking Macaulay out of the frame did just that."

Curtis yawned, raised her legs a little higher and the skirt fell further back. "Life's a bitch."

"I reckon. That's why we're taking you for a ride around Brixton."

Her back came off the bench so quickly it almost took her breath away, "What're you playin' at, man? You know I can't go there."

"You'll be in protective police custody. Mowatt and I will see to it that no harm comes to you while we wander around the market."

"You couldn't stop a gang of them getting me!"

"You know that we'll try, Mona."

"You're not taking me there, I won't go!" She swung her legs off the bench and quickly rose to her feet, backing against a wall.

"You're going, and when we're there we'll make a bit of a fuss so people are sure to notice us."

"You can't." Her arms curled around herself and her statuesque figure shook with an involuntary shudder.

"What's the matter, Mona, cold?"

"You can't take me there. I'll . . . . I'll scream, I'll tell everyone what you're doing before we leave here!"

"Good idea, the more noise you make the more you'll be noticed."

Suddenly she was desperate, as she had been at Notting Hill when waiting for Fisher's men to arrive. Ignoring the detective she paced the floor, obviously agitated by the threatened journey. Then slowly her expression altered and she turned towards him, her huge breasts rising and falling beneath the thin fabric of her T shirt. "Look, maybe we misunderstood one another. I mean, isn't there something else that I can offer to do for you?"

137

"You know what I want, Mona."

She dragged the T shirt over her head and threw it on the floor. A half-cup bra spilled over with dark, succulent flesh that tightened as she reached behind to release a catch. A quick shake of her shoulders was all it took for her pendulous breasts to swing free as the bra fell away. "I've never done it in a cell before, but be my guest."

"Put them away, Mona." He remained on the bench, a fixed idea in his head. "Where's Debbie Ash?"

"I won't say nuthin' if you want to play a little," his eyes told her that she was wasting time. She sighed and stuck out her hip, "What if I don't know where she is?"

"You'd better know."

She collected the T shirt and bra off the floor and put them back on. "She made me promise not to tell. I don't want her to hate me, I still love her."

"Then you won't mind dying for her?"

"You're a cold bastard, aren't you Kinnaird?"

"Live a little longer, Mona, tell me where she is?"

A moment later she did just that. He wrote down the address of a West Indian club in Brixton, made her repeat it to ensure that he had it right, then warned her of the consequences if she had lied, and left her to cry.

Kinnaird found Mowatt in the DI's office, and told them both what he had been able to discover. Evans grimaced and put a question to him. "Is she's telling the truth?"

"She's scared, people usually do when they're like that."

"Before you go steaming in there get on to the local nick and find out what you can about the address," Evans allowed some smoke to escape from one side of his mouth while a cigar hung opposite. "West Indian clubs are notoriously hostile to the law, and we don't want to start a riot, do we, Del?"

"Will you want to come with us?"

"Believe it. Why should you have all the fun?"

Kinnaird turned towards the door expecting Mowatt to follow, but she remained seated in front of the DI's desk.

"It's OK, Del. She and I have a few things to discuss. You can handle what's required alone, can't you?"

He nodded, glanced at Mowatt but didn't find any answers in her eyes. When she finally joined him he was at his desk, the checks on the West Indian club spread out in front of him. What he had found out had been expected. The "Jamaica" was located behind the Railton Road, and served as a collection point for drug traffickers, addicts, thieves, whores and anyone else who enjoyed operating outside the law. All officers were advised not to visit the club without first informing the duty officer at Brixton, and strictly never with fewer than a dozen other officers in attendance.

"Did you discover anything interesting?" Mowatt asked as she pulled up a chair alongside.

"Only that the place is a snakepit. The locals have been considering raiding it for sometime, but the top brass are concerned about repercussions."

"It's to be expected in Brixton."

He shrugged and rose from the chair. "I'm taking the club news to Colin Evans, are you coming?"

"He told me that you're still not happy having me as a partner. I thought we were beginning to understand each other?"

"I can't help the way I feel." He had guessed she and Evans had been discussing their relationship. Something about the way she looked had told him.

"Evans suggested that I ignore you and keep my head down. He also said that I should only wear jeans, to help you forget that I'm a woman."

"Jeans won't hide the fact that you're a woman. That's one of the dumbest things I ever heard."

"Maybe, but I'm going to change. I won't be long."

She pushed up from the chair and he watched her walk down to the door and step out of the office. She had good legs, he thought, as she disappeared.

When Evans heard what Brixton's collator had said about the "Jamaica" club, his enthusiasm lost some of its earlier sparkle. He gave Kinnaird explicit instructions to do nothing until he had discussed the matter with the DCI. The next time Kinnaird saw him his enthusiasm was all but gone, "George Ship says no way, Del. You can forget searching for Debbie Ash if she's hiding in that rat hole. He called Brixton's DCI, apparently they've plans to raid the place very soon and don't want us stepping in too early."

Kinnaird had guessed what Ship's reaction would be, yet wished just once he could have been proved wrong. "How about me going for a look alone?"

"That'd be a hundred times worse, the idea is to avoid creating a war zone."

"Alone, I'm hardly likely to cause a riot."

"You underestimate yourself, we don't. The answer's no. If you're desperate to become a statistic, go walk under a bus, it'd cause less trouble."

"I've been in worse places, Colin."

"I'll say this just once, Kinnaird. Keep away from that club, if you don't you're out, and I mean right out!" Neither of them had heard the DCI enter the office.

Kinnaird looked round, unimpressed by the threat. "What about solving these murders? I thought that was a priority. Debbie Ash is the best lead we have!"

"You say, find yourself another!"

"Easier said than done, but I guess you've forgotten how tough it is out there. It must be a long time since you felt a collar."

Colin Evans stared up at the ceiling as if wishing that he were not there. Ship glowered. "Push your luck any further, Kinnaird, and you can get out now."

"Let's go see what's happening in the squad office, Del." The DI grabbed the detective's arm and led him away before he could voice another antagonistic reply. Out of Ship's sight, a rush of anger spilled out of Evans. "You know better than to do something like that, what the hell got into you?"

"I'm tired of pricks like him telling me what to do. He wants arrests but can't stomach the aggro they bring with them."

"Well, for your information, he's not alone. Why don't you try finding an easy answer to problems instead of charging at each of them like a bull at a gate?"

"Because I want to get a result, and there aren't any easy answers to this one, Colin. Besides, it upset me that we lost that sprog, Bonner. At the time I thought it upset you?"

"It did, but I'm too old to lose any sleep over such things anymore. Look at what happens when we catch scum like this, they get life and are out in fifteen, maybe less. What's the point? The sprog's still dead."

Kinnaird stopped and snatched his arm free. "I'm sorry to hear you talk like that, Colin. Because out of all the brass hats in this place I always gave you credit for being someone with real understanding for what's happening on the streets."

Evans dug his hands deep into his pockets as the weight of responsibilities crept into his tired eyes.

"That's easy for you to say, but in here I need to see things from both sides. Sure you're good on the streets, maybe the best, but in here there's another world to confront, and I'm your spokesman. Like it or not we all have to survive the politics."

"What you're missing is that the politics are taking over priority from the streets. The management are so busy watching their own backs they're actually aiding the villains."

Evans sighed, remembering when he felt the same, long before his promotion to inspector. "I guess everyone's under pressure but then, if you can't take it, you shouldn't have joined."

"I've still got my priorities right, Colin. I'm going to find these killers, and I don't give a damn about Ship!"

"You're headed for a fall, Del. If you don't listen to good advice no one is going to be able to save you."

"At least you warned me, Colin." He turned away. "Your conscience is clear."

A uniformed constable raced up the stairs at the end of the corridor, and paused in front of Kinnaird as he spotted the Inspector. "Excuse me, sir, you're wanted in the squad room. It's urgent. Another prostitute's been attacked."

Mowatt met them on the stairs. "Del, I heard it come over the radio. I know the location."

Kinnaird pushed her ahead of him towards the station yard where their car was parked. As he drove, she gave him a commentary on what she had heard. "The victim's been servicing workmen at a building site in Munster Road for a few weeks. A couple of her regular punters stumbled on to her being attacked about twenty minutes ago. They called an ambulance. She's still alive."

"How many attackers?"

"Just one, but he got away in a car driven by a woman, and no one got a registration."

"Getting bloody confident aren't they? This is the first daylight attack." When they reached the building site Kinnaird parked behind a patrol car. A small crowd of workmen surrounded a uniformed officer who was taking notes. The men who had stumbled on to the attack were heavy set with broad shoulders and bull necks. It came as no surprise that the attacker had fled when they had appeared. The detectives listened to what the men had to say to the uniformed constable then Kinnaird threw in a few questions of his own.

"Are you certain the driver of the getaway car was a woman?"

"No doubt about it, mate," one replied. "Long red hair she had, reached right across her shoulders. Nice looking piece too, I'd say."

"We missed your description of the man, would you mind repeating it for us?"

"Big sod, tall, must've been around six six, and he wore a balaclava and an army-type jacket, y'know, all camouflaged."

"Did you notice anything else about him?"

"Only the knife he was holding, bleeding great thing it was too. I reckon poor Jenny would've been dog meat if we hadn't turned up, not that he ran away immediately he saw us. It was only when we started lobbing bricks at him that he got the message."

"Can you tell us anything else about the woman?"

"Not apart from her red hair," the workman shrugged, then added, "The getaway motor was a Cortina Ghia, dark blue. I know it was a Ghia 'cos of the wheels, smart set of alloys it had. It went off towards New King's Road."

Kinnaird and Mowatt returned to the car, deep in thought. As she looked across from her seat she said, "They're getting relaxed about this aren't they? I mean the attacker only fled when bricks were thrown at him."

"Maybe, or perhaps they're just trying to tighten the screws on Duffy's whores. A daylight attack like this is going to cause a lot of panic."

She sighed, "And we're no closer to finding them."

He shrugged, grim-faced, and drove south towards the New King's Road with her glancing in his direction, wishing he would talk. "This is a pretty tough relationship we've got, Kinnaird. One minute I think we're getting along then something happens and pow, we're back to square one."

"Maybe I'm not having a good day but if it's too tough, you know the answer . . . . "

"Yeah, yeah." She ignored his remark, and abruptly realised that she wouldn't have done so only a few days ago. Things had really changed. "Do you think the red-head could be Sonny Fisher? From a distance it would be hard to distinguish a man dressed like a woman."

"It's possible, if Fisher can be described as good looking." Kinnaird became distant, wondering about the identity of the man called Hastings, and his importance in the vice war scenario. Since Fisher had become a known player in events, it looked as if Debbie Ash had deliberately lied about Macaulay. If that were true then it was equally likely that she knew Hastings' real identity. Arresting Fisher could help, but only if they had grounds to hold him. He doubted Mona Curtis would now support her earlier allegation that Fisher had contracted the attack on her. However Fisher could be arrested on suspicion of being involved in the attacks on Duffy's prostitutes, especially if he wore red hair. Kinnaird shook his head, disagreeing with himself. That would only work if they had something concrete to threaten Fisher. No matter how hard he tried looking for answers to resolve their problems, he kept returning to Debbie Ash as the key.

"What are you thinking?" Mowatt dragged him back from his thoughts.

"Just wondering who Hastings really is."

"Does it matter? He's probably just a heavy hired by Fisher." She saw the doubt written all over his face. "Why do I get the feeling that you don't agree?"

"Hastings has been important from the start, he must be, because he's been trying hard to hide his identity. Sheenarena knew him, so did Tina Wilson and her pimp. Now they're dead. That makes him very important, probably someone with a high profile."

"If you're right then all we've got to do is work out who else might know him."

"I've already worked that out – Duffy. Lenny Jones told me that he did 'the Man' a favour once, and I've had a hard time trying to imagine what Jones could have offered someone like Duffy. Now I think I know."

"If you're right, then perhaps Fisher and Hastings are a partnership. If Jones did know Hastings' identity and told Duffy, that makes 'The Man' a target too."

"It also makes finding Debbie Ash even more crucial." He turned the car towards the river.

"But we don't have permission to go to Brixton," she replied uneasily, recognising a determined look in his eyes that had nothing to do with orders. "I don't like what you're thinking, Del."

"We do as I say, remember, that was one of the rules!"

"You're putting your job on the line, why do you always

have to do that?" A shrug of his broad shoulders was his only reply. "Look, there're only two of us, shouldn't we at least get some back up, there's strength in numbers?"

"We don't need anyone else. All you have to do is wait for me in the car. If I don't return within a half-hour then call the cavalry."

"What do you take me for? I'm not sitting in the car while you're being murdered, I'm coming in with you!"

"You can't save my life by coming in with me, but you might by calling for help. You must be able to see the sense that makes."

"If Greg Wright were here instead of me, you'd take him inside!"

"No I wouldn't," the lie came easily and stopped her argument. He had guessed that she would resist his plan, would want to remain at his side no matter what the danger. He also well understood her feelings, because he had experienced them himself as a probationer. What he wasn't certain about was whether she could wait the full thirty minutes for him to return. A person's imagination played all kinds of tricks when someone's life was in peril, and Mowatt was the protective kind. He recognised that because it was something else they shared. Yet if she came alone to his rescue, he doubted either of them would survive to tell about it. "If anything goes wrong, I want you to promise me that you'll make the call for help instead of trying to get me out on your own."

She folded her arms and didn't speak.

Six

The West Indian club was a detached single-storey building located between two rows of terraced houses. About a hundred years ago it had been constructed as a chapel, somewhere for people to worship the almighty, but that purpose had passed away long ago. Today its stone walls were decorated in vivid yellows and purples, while a bright red sign hung over a double door entrance with the name Jamaica written in fancy lettering. Kinnaird drove passed and parked a block away.

"It was just how I imagined it," Mowatt shuddered, but not from cold. "Except no one seemed to be around. I suppose you're still determined to go it alone?"

"Don't worry, I'm not really suicidal. See you in thirty minutes." Kinnaird climbed out of the car and headed back towards the club. Mowatt leaned an arm over the seat-back and stared out of the rear screen, unhappy as she watched him disappear around a corner.

He found the club's double doors closed but unlocked and stepped inside. The only light filtered in through half-a-dozen grimy windows still painted with depictions of saints, but it was enough to see the place was empty. In the centre sat a circular bar surrounded on all sides by tables and chairs, no carpet. Kinnaird moved further in and met a strong mix of booze and ganja, invisible companions in the

147

dry atmosphere, the ganja so strong his head tingled. When he reached the bar he found it well stocked with drink, an open invitation to any walk-in thief, but the cash register had been emptied. On the far side, opposite the entrance, sat four doors, two of them easy to identify because of the word Toilet painted in green. He pushed open an unmarked door and found a shabby bedroom, no more than eight by six. A single bed with stained sheets occupied most of the available space beneath a dirty window. A bucket of used condoms sat beside the bed, while a stench in the air seemed even less acceptable to breathe than the booze and ganja. It was the same in the next room, no people, just a bed and bucket of used condoms. Kinnaird felt disappointed. He had wanted to find Debbie Ash, but guessed Mona Curtis had steered him here hoping he wouldn't return. She hadn't counted on the place being empty. Suddenly the distinctive tones of a West Indian accent emanated from outside the bedroom. Kinnaird pushed the door almost closed and stared through a narrow gap as people began to emerge from a hole in the floor behind the bar.

"What d'you mean it ain't enough? That's the goin' rate you've been paid. I can't help it if the cold is keeping people away!" A man with a Rastafarian hairstyle climbed up through the hole in the floor and stepped out from the bar followed by a tall, broad shouldered red-head wearing a fur coat and strapless high heels.

"Just as long as we understand one another, Jerry." The red-head spoke with a menacing, deep resonant voice that sounded as if it belonged to a man.

"I don't do things like that, because I don't want no trouble with Sonny Fisher!" The West Indian held his hands up in front of him as if pleading to be believed.

Another figure suddenly popped up through the floor, a small blonde wearing a black mini-dress with a coat slung over her arm. Debbie Ash.

Fisher leaned on the bar. "That's good. Then you won't mind if Deb stays over for a few days free of charge?"

"How long's a few days?"

"Till I say it's safe for her to come out. The old bill are scouring London trying to find her."

The West Indian studied the young woman. "Is she willing to work? I'd have plenty of customers who'd pay well for the privilege, me included."

"Forget it!" she snapped with a firm shake of her head.

"You heard her, Jerry, and I don't want to find out that you or any of your customers tried it on with her. She said no, and that's final. She remains here until I say otherwise."

"Is she really that hot?"

"It doesn't concern you what she is, just keep her out of sight."

"OK, Sonny. I'll go down and straighten the place up a bit." The West Indian disappeared into the hole behind the bar.

"Sonny, how long do you expect me to stay in this pigsty?"

"You've got Duffy and the law chasing you, what do you think? We're almost where we want to be, it'd be a shame to lose it all now. Just a couple more weeks is all we need."

"D'you really think Duffy will just give up?"

"His girls are pissed off, some have even moved out of London. I've taken on thirty myself this week. He can't survive much longer, and there's not a thing he can do about it."

"Can you trust this bloke, Jerry?"

"As much as I can anyone. He knows better than to trouble you. And you're safe from the law. They won't come here in case it starts a riot."

As the West Indian re-emerged, four black youths raced excitedly into the club. Their leader, a tall, gangly eighteen-year-old, blatantly leered at Debbie Ash as he led the others towards the bar. "Hey, Jerry, we've found something outside which you should see."

"It's cold out there, and I'm busy, Lewis. I don't have time to play guessing games, if you've got somethin' tell me."

"You're gonna wanna see it, Jerry."

The West Indian shook his head and stepped out from behind the bar, "You're going to feel pain if this is a waste of time, Lewis!"

They crowded out through the entrance with Fisher and Debbie Ash trailing. Kinnaird checked the time, ten minutes remained before Mowatt called for help. He had accomplished finding the girl and could wait for a more opportune moment to pick her up. A bedroom window opened on to a narrow drive which ran past the back of the club. He followed it to a street then headed back to his car, excited and pleased. When he turned the corner the first thing he noticed was that the Capri was empty. He rushed forward, found it locked with the ignition keys missing. Tentacles of trouble crept over him, the excited black youths and Mowatt's disappearance irrevocably linked. She couldn't wait, had gone to the club to check on him, and been captured. It was the only explanation. He kept a spare key in his wallet, unlocked the car door and drove back to the club feeling like he was operating on automatic, not thinking, simply reacting to circumstances. As he parked opposite the club and climbed out, the black youth named Lewis erupted from its entrance howling for Kinnaird's blood, closely followed by a pack of wild friends. The detective jumped back into the car and spun the V6 engine into life as snarling faces reached his door, suddenly disappearing as he floored the accelerator and raced away. He stopped a hundred yards on while behind him the young black men congregated in the middle of the road, a pack of wolves on the scent of a kill. He shifted the automatic into reverse, turned to look out through the rear screen, mumbled something about 'no-go areas', and pushed the accelerator down for a second time. The pack scattered in every direction, yelling, leaping and diving out of his way. Kinnaird braked hard, tyres screeching, and a youth sprang on to the bonnet wielding an ugly, long blade. A malevolent grin spread across the detective's face as the youth growled and raised the knife high into the air, then shot over the roof as the Capri rocketed forward. When he stopped again another of the pack charged the car. Kinnaird's door flew open and a blade stabbed at him. He caught the youth's wrist and kept the knife away from his chest as he punched the accelerator. The Capri shot forward and the youth suddenly lost interest in murdering him while his short legs worked hard to keep up with the car. The knife fell from his hand, his angry eyes suddenly anxious as he blubbered about not wanting to die, then Kinnaird released him. He cartwheeled a dozen times before thudding into the side of a parked van. The Capri rolled to a stop and the detective looked around for the remainder of the pack. They had congregated at club's entrance, away from the road. He U-turned and pointed the Capri's nose towards them while they shouted and gestured, urging him to take his chances out of the car. Only Mowatt's predicament didn't make it a stalemate, Kinnaird had to act. The Capri was fitted with a pair of Maserati air horns which had a decibel rating that easily overwhelmed the legal limit. The detective could think of no better way of gaining the attention of the people in the neighbouring houses, and leaned a palm on the horn. The blast of noise initially startled the youths, but they were quick to appreciate what he had in mind. A shower of stones peppered the car until he was forced to release the horn to back out of range.

When he stopped and was about to experiment with the horn again the club doors burst open. Fisher and the West Indian strode out with Mowatt gripped between them. Debbie Ash tagged on behind. Even from a distance Mowatt looked pale. They stopped briefly, spoke to the pack, and the blonde rushed across the road and climbed in behind the wheel of a big black Vauxhall. Ash turned it around to point away from Kinnaird, and Mowatt was crammed into the back. The pack split up, some raced towards Kinnaird, their hands full of stones, while the West Indian led another group towards a van. The detective ignored them, his attention focused on the Vauxhall with Mowatt as Fisher joined her. A hail of stones suddenly beat the ground around the Capri, bouncing high and smacking the sides of the car like shrapnel from a grenade. The attempted distraction didn't work. Kinnaird spotted a couple more youths climb into the Vauxhall making it full of people, but even then it sat waiting for something more to happen. The van driven by the West Indian swung across the road – the something the Vauxhall had been waiting for, and Mowatt was driven away. The Capri snarled as it bounced on to the kerb and stormed alongside a row of terraced houses. From the corner of his eye the detective saw the van move, a big square mass of metal that lumbered along ahead and to the right of him. The Capri charged onwards, quickly building up speed. The van would soon be a memory. Then the mass of metal jumped on to the kerb ahead between a couple of parked cars. Kinnaird slammed the brake pedal, the car slewed sideways and stopped abruptly as it banged into the van. Kinnaird threw the shift into reverse, and the rear wheels spun enthusiastically as the Capri launched itself back on to the road. The van did the same, keeping its nose pointed towards the detective's car. The West Indian gave Kinnaird no time to do anything other than reverse while the van chased him, bumping the Capri's front bumper as a reminder he was there. The detective steered, looking over his shoulder through the rear screen, whilst jeered at by his pursuers as if he were already finished. A straight stretch of road suddenly loomed up and Kinnaird stabbed the accelerator. The Capri grunted, as if in relief, and sped away in reverse, distancing itself from the van. At the end of the straight a slow bend rushed up to meet him. Kinnaird backed off the power and let the Capri glide backwards around it, then braked hard to avoid hitting a wall that constituted a dead end. The van came around the bend, still in pursuit. The detective pushed the shift into drive and hit the accelerator one more time. As the speedometer's needle rushed around to fifty miles an hour, Kinnaird opened the car door. When the distance from the van was fewer than twenty feet he threw himself out, curling into a tight ball that rolled away across the road. An eternity passed as the world around him became a dizzy, whirling picture, then the blast of an explosion rolled him further and further on until he thought he would never stop. But he did, finally, and registered a second explosion, a louder one. He blacked out. Moments later he resurfaced, face down in a gutter, his entire body racked with pain, but miraculously nothing was broken. He managed to push himself onto his knees as a patrol car swung around the bend.

Kinnaird was taken to a local hospital, patched up and returned to Fulham. He stood in the DCI's office, the shoulder-pads of his jacket torn, his trousers gashed, his face bruised and cut, his body aching. He reported Mowatt's kidnap to both George Ship and Colin Evans. What they were thinking behind grave expressions did not require telepathy. They allowed him to finish before the DCI broke into a brief, tense silence.

"You disobeyed a direct order by going to that club." It came out cool and detached, just like the man. "By doing so you've placed a colleague's life in very real danger, and caused the deaths of three men."

"They were attempting to kill me."

"You leave me no choice," the DCI ignored him. "You're suspended from duty as of now to await disciplinary proceedings. Give me your warrant card."

"Don't you think that we should forgo the formalities until we get Mel back, then you can do whatever you want with me?"

The DCI studied him briefly, and some of his usual detachment faltered. "Your inflated ego is what gets you and everyone around you into trouble, Kinnaird. Do you really think that you're the only one who can find her?" George Ship rose slowly to his feet, "Well I've news for you, there are at least a dozen blokes in your office just as capable. In fact, they wouldn't have lost her in the first place. Now drop your warrant card on my desk and get out!"

Kinnaird stepped out of the office escorted by Evans and headed towards the exit, "You asked for that, Del. I warned you what would happen but you wouldn't listen."

"Right now I don't give a damn, Colin. I just want to get Mel back."

"You can't mean you're going after her alone?"

"I'm the only one with a chance of finding her alive, no matter what Ship says!"

"For Christ's sake, keep out of it. You're off the case. You're not even a copper anymore!"

"Good, that means I've a free hand to play by their rules." Evans grabbed his arm, "If you mess up again there won't be any chance of your getting back in, think about it."

"If I mess up again that'll be the least of my worries." He snatched his arm free and strode away.

Kinnaird's immediate requirement after leaving the station was for new transport. He hired Ford's latest small car, a Fiesta, from a local garage at Parson's Green. It came supplied with a full tank of four star fuel, which at 73p a gallon, brought the total bill to a little over thirty-five pounds for a week. If he lost his job he speculated on how long it would be before he found another, and questioned whether he should be spending almost a third of a week's basic pay on transport. Perhaps Evans had been right and he should stay out of it? Yet the haunting memory of Mowatt, caught because she was concerned for him, refused to disappear. Also a hire car was essential for what he had in mind. He could have borrowed a car, but this way he avoided getting friends involved. The economics of life were brushed aside as he determined that there was no other way.

He drove to the Roma restaurant for another talk with Duffy. The place was almost empty when he arrived, and 'The Man', ever cautious, sat eating with his back to a wall in a corner from which he could watch the entrance. One of his men sat with him. When the detective stopped in front of his table the vice king gave a wide grin.

"You really should find yourself a decent tailor, Kinnaird, those cheap suits don't last." The detective had not changed his clothes since jumping from his car in Brixton.

"I want Fisher and Debbie Ash, and you can point me in the right direction."

"I'll say this for you, Kinnaird. You've plenty of front. I'm not so sure about brains though. D'you really expect me to help you?"

"Why shouldn't you?"

"I hate your guts for one!"

"This is business. Also, it's mutually beneficial."

"I've never required help from a pig, and I especially don't need anything you've on offer. For a start, take a look at yourself, you're washed up, Kinnaird, a has-been. You were so cocky about the next time you ran into who you were chasing, you believed your own press, but things didn't work out the way you thought. They beat you again, and I'd say they made a pretty good job of it. So why don't you just go away and leave real men to sort this out."

"Fisher got away, but I left three of his men dead. I'm still the best, Duffy, but I'm wondering about you, and whether you've become such a fat cat that you've lost the balls to do more than spit words. You're in trouble, and don't give me any shit about being able to take care of things. I overheard Fisher discussing what's happening here with Debbie. If I go out of that door empty handed, he's going to steamroller you out of business, and you know it!"

The vice king lost his grin, took a little time thinking over what Kinnaird had said, then told the man at his table to go for a walk. He pushed the plate of food in front of him away as if it suddenly disgusted him. The detective sat down, and was thankful for a chance to do so. "OK, what're you offering, Kinnaird?"

"To stop Fisher once and for all."

Duffy lit a cigarette without saying anything, but his eyes never left the detective's face. "Fisher made you that mad, eh?"

"I want to know about Debbie Ash. How'd she get so close to Fisher?" Kinnaird waited for Duffy to reply, but he smoked his cigarette without providing any answers. "Did she leave you because she knew Fisher had it in him to push you off the top?"

"She ain't that stupid."

"She ain't stupid, period. So why'd she leave you for him, weren't you paying her enough?"

He began to grow another grin, one that looked crooked and made him remove the cigarette from his mouth.

"That's for me to know and you to wonder."

"She still works for you, doesn't she?" It came out more as a thought than a question. "That's how you've been able to keep tabs on him, and the reason up until now that you've been feeling smug with yourself. You're just waiting for Debbie Ash to tell you the right moment to hit back, but it's not working out exactly how you planned is it?"

"She's upset because Fisher's boys almost reached Mona, but she'll get over it. Besides Mona needed a lesson. She was getting too many ideas above her station and needed a slap down."

"What are you giving Debbie in return for this help? And don't tell me she's doing it for love, not that one."

"You're wrong, Kinnaird. Apart from a fat cheque, she wants Mona Curtis. But don't look so surprised, they've been together a long time." He stabbed out the cigarette in an ashtray and leaned back on the chair. "You're right, thanks to Debbie I know every move that Fisher makes, and when he goes for the big one I'll be ready."

"Even without Macaulay?"

"That was Debbie's revenge for my not looking after her girlfriend, though I doubt she thought that you'd go round there and shoot him. Count yourself lucky that he's not dead, otherwise you'd have had a contract out on you."

"Spare me the threats. When did you last hear from Debbie?"

"You're worried about your pretty partner, eh?" He saw the surprise in Kinnaird's eyes and laughed. "I told you that she keeps me informed with what's happening. Your partner's safe for the moment, though she's got too much to say for herself."

"Where is she?"

"It's not that easy, Kinnaird. I still appear to hold all the aces. Fisher won't win."

"But you're interested in letting me stop Fisher otherwise I wouldn't still be here. I'll do it permanently without you getting involved; that should hold plenty of appeal from where you're sitting."

"You're suspended, how're you gonna do that and get away with it?" Kinnaird's face showed his surprise, and Duffy gloated. "I've snouts everywhere, that's how I've survived at the top for so long."

"There are snouts and there are snouts, but that information is hot off the press." Kinnaird wondered if it were be possible to find out how many people were aware of his suspension, then work out which of them might have told Duffy. Unfortunately he didn't have the time. "I'm still a cop, and that shithead kidnapped a cop. Therefore my killing Fisher when I save my partner won't be looked at as anything other than legal homicide." Kinnaird had no intention of murdering Sonny Fisher, but knew offering to do so was the carrot to prise the information he needed from Duffy. "I also want the bloke calling himself Hastings."

"The cash clout," the vice king slipped another cigarette into his mouth, lit it, then blew out a cloud of smoke. "His name isn't Hastings, but then I think you've already guessed that."

"Thrill me, what's his real name?"

"Not so fast. I'll give you Fisher, maybe. But the other one, what will you give me for him?"

"I make certain he goes to the cells with Fisher, leaving you without any competition, isn't that enough?"

"Without Fisher I doubt he'd bother me. It's not as if he needs the wedge, he's got plenty of that all ready."

"So what do you want?"

"I almost forgot, you also get your girlfriend back when I tell you where to find Fisher. You do pretty well out of this don't you?"

"Just tell me what you want, Duffy?"

"You to work for me. I pay well."

"Doing what?"

"Not much really. Help me out when I ask. Keep me informed when any of my businesses are going to receive police attention."

"You've already got someone working for you at the station, why d'you need me?"

"You're in the CID."

Kinnaird could not imagine Duffy really expecting him to agree, and yet, 'The Man' had asked. Perhaps he thought Kinnaird desperate enough to do anything, possibly because of Mowatt, possibly because Kinnaird had been suspended.

Duffy might think him bitter towards the police as a whole. But even if he did agree, Kinnaird was curious how Duffy expected to enforce their agreement once Mowatt was free. All the detective could be certain was that Duffy did nothing without looking at the long-term implications. "You can't really expect me to agree to something like that?"

"Why not? This has nothing to do with how I feel about you, it's business. From where I'm sitting you don't look to be in good shape. You might lose your job without my help. On top of that your partner could wind up dead."

"What else?"

Duffy laughed, "I'll come clean. If you're working for me, you won't be such a pain in the arse as you are at the moment.

"And how do you stop me from reneging on any deal?"

"Simple. You care about other people more than you do about yourself. If you renege on me, someone you love gets hurt. I mean seriously hurt."

An impulse to drag him across the table made Kinnaird's hands flex momentarily. Duffy meant it, and Vienna was the obvious target. "If anything like that were to happen. I'd kill you."

"No. You'd try." He took the cigarette out of his mouth and propped it against the side of an ashtray, letting it burn, the smoke rising into Kinnaird's eyes.

Duffy was close to achieving something he had never dreamed possible. Kinnaird had hounded his business for years and now, quite suddenly, he had the opportunity to stop Kinnaird without repercussions. Several times in the past he had considered murdering the detective, but the thought of an intensive investigation, with him as the major suspect, made him resist. "So what d'you say detective? Do you want to know where to find your partner or not? She won't live for much longer."

Kinnaird knew he would renege. The same as he knew he would have to come after Duffy once Mowatt was safe.

"I guess you've a new employee."

"I don't expect you to sound overjoyed, but you could at least unclench your teeth." Duffy stared at the cigarette burning without assistance. "Coming after me won't save Vienna. I thought you should know that."

"You like to live on the edge, don't you?"

"Same as you." He picked the cigarette up and put it back between his lips. "No one reneges on a deal with me once it's made. I promise Kinnaird, if you do, you'll wish you'd never been born."

"Thrill me, what's Hastings' real name?"

"Sir Alexander Hodgkiss." It came as close to a thrill as Duffy could ever get.

"The newspaper tycoon. No wonder he's been trying to keep his identity secret."

"You've heard of him," the other man sneered. "Now you know how Fisher was able to move so quickly in taking over the south's vice rackets. Hodgkiss generates so much capital he could pay off the national debt."

"But how did someone like Hodgkiss get involved with a sleaze ball like Sonny Fisher, they're not exactly operating in the same field?" Sir Alexander Hodgkiss was a self-made millionaire, and the owner of two powerful Fleet Street tabloids. The newspapers, like their owner, were biased towards Conservatism, and could always be counted on to condemn the Labour government. Yet Hodgkiss was much more than simply a newspaper tycoon, his wealth stretched into property, oil and pharmaceuticals, while his charisma and lowly beginnings had turned him into something of a national hero, the kind of man people looked up to and respected.

"Sex. Hodgkiss is bisexual, and a sadist to boot. They were made for one another. They met at a party more than a year ago and have been bosom pals ever since." Duffy blew more clouds of smoke into the air and came forward on his chair. "Hodgkiss isn't the kind you can simply blow away, Kinnaird. Not even you."

"But you're saying that he's responsible for the beatings and murders?" The detective fixed on Duffy's gaze as the vice king's head nodded in agreement. He was hoping to spot something that suggested 'The Man' was lying to him, as Debbie Ash had done, but Duffy was smugly genuine, because they both realised that it would take much more than the word of a vice king or a suspended detective to bring a charge of murder against someone like Hodgkiss. For that reason he believed Duffy and, knowing 'The Man', guessed he would have made it his business to discover the vulnerabilities of any rival, including one occupying such an elevated position in the community. "So what, apart from sex, is his weakness?"

"Fisher's involved with a group of druggies down in Brixton. They congregate at a club called the Jamaica."

"Them I met."

"I don't believe Hodgkiss knows about the links between the druggies and Fisher. It could seriously damage the great man's standing if someone first exposed his connection to Fisher, then Fisher's to the druggies. It's something I've been working on."

"Why do I get the feeling this is where Debbie Ash comes in?"

"Hodgkiss became infatuated with her, she saw to that. There aren't many who could've captured his attention the way she did. I'm told they have some pretty wild threesome parties."

"But how certain of Debbie are you? She strikes me as the kind who'd want a lot more than a fat cheque and Mona Curtis. Hodgkiss could offer her that?"

"You're reading her wrong, Kinnaird. She values Mona Curtis more than anything else, and that includes money."

The vice king stabbed out the cigarette, and watched a thin whisp of smoke rise towards the ceiling. "They're welcome to one another as far as I'm concerned. Mona's the toughest main bitch that ever worked for me, but she's got a screw loose, and that makes her dangerous."

"She never struck me as tougher than any of the other girls working for you." Kinnaird recalled how she had appeared at Notting Hill while waiting for Fisher's gunmen, then again in the cell when he had threatened her with a journey to Brixton.

"She'd fool anyone, even you. I'm telling you, she doesn't have a nerve in her body."

"OK, you told me, but why is Fisher so determined to keep her away from Debbie?"

"Because of Hodgkiss. Sonny Fisher's got a good thing going with Debbie as the great man's plaything. He even forked out five grand to keep Mona over here. The bitch took it but couldn't keep to her end of the deal. Hence the contract on her. I didn't mind that she ripped Fisher off, but she should've remembered me when she took the cash. That's history now though, she's back in line."

"I still have trouble imagining someone like Hodgkiss slitting throats."

"I told you that he's a sadist. He enjoys beating women and simply graduated to killing them. I don't see your problem."

Kinnaird shrugged like it was unimportant, but inwardly

163

he sensed its significance. In the same way that identifying the killer's female/male partner was significant. It was a missing piece of the puzzle. In his eyes a sadist might graduate from paying women to be beaten to attacking them on the streets, thereby receiving an additional thrill for the risk. Slitting throats was something else. "Thanks for the info, now where do I find Fisher?"

"D'you think you can deal with Fisher and Hodgkiss?"

"I'm going to try."

"Is that new partner of yours more than just a workmate?"

"She's someone I feel responsible for . . . "

"Nasty, Kinnaird," Duffy shook his head. "Very nasty, dangerous too. Shows you've a conscience. I've never been able to afford such a luxury."

"But then we've always been on opposite sides."

"Till now."

Kinnaird rose to his feet, "It's make your mind up time, are you going to give me that address or what?"

"Thirty, Stanley Road, West Croydon. It's a small two-bed semi. Fisher has a thing about not living in style. Apparently the taxman scares the shit out of him. He reckons the Inland Revenue is a million times worse than the old bill, but you're all the same to me. You should've been put down at birth."

"You don't really mean that, Duffy, you'd have missed the challenge."

"I could live with the loss. What're you intending to do about Hodgkiss?"

"I'll see if I can dig up someone to point a finger at him for the murders. It should be easier now that I know who he is."

"Leave Debbie and Mona out of it, they wouldn't talk anyway, not without my backing."

Kinnaird nodded and walked away.

Stanley Road, West Croydon was a narrow tree-lined thoroughfare made narrower by a multitude of parked cars spread alongside either of its opposing kerbs. Most houses in the road were thirties two-bedroomed semis that appeared well maintained, and somehow managed to cling to a country air that had no right to exist in a suburb of London. Number thirty was pebble-dashed and painted white with a shared drive running to a garage at the back. Outside its front door sat a big black Vauxhall. Kinnaird rolled past the house in the hire car, his coat collar up helping the dark, dismal evening prevent him being easily recognisable. An upstairs light showed behind a thin veil of curtain, while the remainder of the house belonged to the darkness. Kinnaird parked in a side road outside a public house. As he climbed out of the car a Hillman Avenger parked behind him, two men climbed out. One stayed by the car the other approached the detective.

"Your name Kinnaird?" A bald, thick set, six footer, a scar running the length of his right cheek, spoke in a high-pitched voice incompatible with his size.

"Who wants to know?"

"Duffy sent us. He thought you might want some help."

"I don't!" The notion that the vice king was concerned for his welfare troubled him. "He said we should give you this." The six-footer handed him a 9mm Browning.

"Is it loaded?" Kinnaird stared at the weapon in his hands, remembering the expression on Duffy's face whenever he had mentioned Sonny Fisher. 'The Man' wanted Fisher dead and was providing the firepower as well as the manpower to ensure that he kept to his side of their deal.

"Not much use otherwise, is it!"

"I only asked because I know Duffy has a queer sense

of humour." He slipped the weapon into a pocket without checking the magazine.

"He told me to tell you that it better be used." The six footer shifted uneasily on the balls of his feet. "I wouldn't wanna be in your shoes if it don't. Know what I mean?"

"Remember not to get in front of it."

The other man grinned, "Duffy said you were a comedian."

"Is that all?"

"We'll be in the car if you need us. Our instructions are to wait till the job's done so that we can confirm the hit." He turned back to the Hillman and Kinnaird strode away towards the house in Stanley Road.

A call box at the end of the road, out of sight of the house gave him an opportunity to check the Browning. Its had a full magazine and was well maintained. He jammed the gun into a coat pocket, stepped out of the call box and headed towards the house, walking straight up to its front door. He used a bell push to gain attention and waited with the wind biting chillingly through his coat.

Debbie Ash opened the front door wearing the friendliest of smiles. "I guessed you'd show up."

"So you're not disappointed." He stepped through the entrance without waiting for an invitation, his hand gripped around the Browning which he kept in his pocket.

"Where is she?"

"Upstairs, follow me." She closed the door and went up a narrow staircase ahead of him, a short black skirt flapping around the tops of her plump thighs. Kinnaird was too hyped up to do more than register the distraction. They reached a small landing and she turned immediately left into a bedroom at the front of the house. Kinnaird hesitated, looked back down the stairs then to his right, but there was no one else. He stepped into the front bedroom and found Mowatt sitting on a bed while Sonny Fisher stood behind her. Debbie Ash occupied a space in front of a fireplace, the only other person there. Fisher wore a tight-fitting blue dress and long red hair, but what caught the detective's attention was a knife he held against Mowatt's throat.

"Take your hands out of your pockets and do it slow, Kinnaird!"

The detective did as he was told, slowly removed his hands from the coat pockets, and shot Fisher. The bullet clipped his shoulder and spun him like a top. The knife flew out of his hand, banged against a chimney breast then clattered to the floor. Mowatt and Ash reached the same decision simultaneously and dived for it. Kinnaird watched as they clawed and pulled one another's hair until Mowatt stopped behaving like a woman and punched the blonde in the mouth. She then collected the knife and turned to Kinnaird.

"You took your damn time finding me!"

"You were meant to stay in the car!" Kinnaird frowned which made her redden with guilt. "You should've at least left a trail. Are you OK?"

"I'll live. Did you bring any backup?"

"Not the kind you're thinking about. Duffy has a couple of his men waiting outside, he sent them along to ensure I waste Fisher. It's a long story, but he and I had a deal which I'm about to renege on."

"I won't even ask, but have you a plan on getting us out of here? Fisher sent his men for some food about twenty minutes ago. They'll be back soon."

"You're finished, man. The others will blow the both of you away." Fisher rose to his feet, a hand covering his shoulder wound.

"Shut your mouth, creep, otherwise I'll equalise your shoulders with this!" Mowatt waved the knife at him. She and Fisher shared a glare then he fell silent. She said, "There isn't a phone so we can't even call for help."

"Duffy's men are watching the front. We'll go out the back and cut across the rear gardens. My car's parked in a side street to our right."

"You can't expect me to climb fences," Fisher nodded at his shoulder. "I need a doctor otherwise I might bleed to death!"

"Promises," Kinnaird glanced at the unconscious blonde lying by the fireplace. "We're not leaving her. Wake her up, Mel."

Mowatt shook Ash awake by the shoulders. Dark blues and purples discoloured her cheek where she had been hit. Gingerly her fingers touched the bruising as Mowatt helped her up off the floor.

"That's some punch you've got, sister," the blonde said, surprising Mowatt with a show of admiration instead of abuse.

"You deserved it," she dragged her towards the stairs with Fisher and Kinnaird bringing up the rear. They moved through the house into a small kitchen and out into a rear garden.

Fisher stared at a wooden fence no more than four and a half feet high and shook his head. "I can't climb that in this skirt!"

"Hike it up around your waist," Kinnaird ordered.

"I'm freezing already, you should've let us get our coats!"

"Either you climb over the fence on your own or you do it with my help?"

Fisher looked into the detective's eyes and saw something that made him pull the skirt up around his waist. The transvestite's underwear amounted to a tan pair of stockings and suspenders, nothing else. Mowatt caught her breath and gawped at the sight of his nakedness while Kinnaird grinned, "Surprised?"

"Only that it's not bigger," she laughed.

"Bitch!" Fisher glared at both of them.

"Start climbing, Sonny. Debbie, give him a hand."

"Let me go, Kinnaird." She stepped towards him. "Duffy's men won't hurt me, you must know that."

"I know, but you and I have some unfinished business to sort out over Macaulay. Now help Fisher over the fence, we don't have much time."

"What're you saying, Deb, why wouldn't Duffy's men hurt you?" Fisher asked, confused, staring at the blonde through suspicious eyes, "Duffy's out to waste you same as me . . . . isn't he?"

"You can talk about it later," Kinnaird told them. "You're staying Debbie, now help Fisher over the fence."

They crossed several gardens without being challenged until a shot rang out and a bullet thudded into a tree close to Kinnaird. They threw themselves flat on the ground then scrambled towards a back door. Mowatt led Debbie Ash and Fisher inside, but Kinnaird remained in the garden long enough to fire a couple of rounds that temporarily stopped Duffy's men chasing them. The detective reached the back door as more shots rang out, but not fired at him. Fisher's youths had returned and a mini war had broken out between them and Duffy's men. Kinnaird raced into the house and caught up with the others as they moved into a hall which ran alongside a staircase. A startled old man stood frozen on the stairs clutching the lapels of his cardigan together. "I'm a pensioner, I don't have any money."

They were on the street before he had time to utter another

plea. Kinnaird led them to the hire car and threw Mowatt the keys. "You drive."

"What this?" She stared at the car as if it were a mistake.

"It's yet another story." He held open the passenger door and Fisher went to climb in but stumbled, crying out as he slammed his wounded shoulder against the back-seat. Kinnaird, momentarily distracted, was struck by a swift knee to the groin. Debbie Ash then ran towards the gunmen emerging from a house. The detective, his eyes watering, his legs buckling, fell into the car and Mowatt sped away.

"Are you all right?"

He nodded, his breath returning, the pain easing.

"Where do you want to take him?" She asked as he leaned over the seat back to check on Fisher's condition.

"Fulham. I don't want to risk losing him to another nick."

"Christ, I'll bleed to death before we get there. I need a hospital!"

Kinnaird handed him a handkerchief, "Keep this over the wound and you probably won't die."

"You bastard!" There was real feeling in the way Fisher used the word. "No nick can keep me, you've no idea what you're up against!"

Kinnaird looked deeply into his eyes. "Saying things like that might make me believe you, and that would be a shame as far as you're concerned."

"You don't scare me, pig!"

"I don't intend letting you get away with what's been happening, Fisher. If I thought you would, I'd kill you now."

The vice-man faltered. Lost for words. The grim sincerity in Kinnaird's eyes told their own story. The detective was certain he had caught a killer.

170

SEVEN

Kinnaird and Mowatt deposited Fisher into the care of a police surgeon at Fulham. Kinnaird then telephoned Vienna and told her to go and stay with Wright's wife until he came to collect her. She didn't argue, simply told him to be careful. He and Mowatt were in the charge room when the DCI, DI and Detective Sergeant Bill Moran found them. Ship temporarily directed his speech at Mowatt and ignored Kinnaird.

"Glad to have you safely back with us, Melanie."

"It's all thanks to DC Kinnaird, sir." She thought she spotted the DCI cringe at mention of her partner's name.

"As I recall he got you into that situation in the first place?"

"Not really, sir. I . . . . "

Ship waved a hand to silence her. "What about this Fisher character, I imagine we should be grateful he's still breathing, considering Kinnaird's history. How bad are his injuries?"

"A flesh wound to the shoulder, sir. Fisher had a knife to my throat when DC Kinnaird shot him."

The DCI finally allowed his gaze to acknowledge Kinnaird, "And where the hell did you get a gun?"

"I found it outside the house they were holding Melanie . . . . sir."

"Convenient for you, careless of them. What about Debbie Ash, was she there?"

171

"She got away, sir," the detective said, noting a crooked smile quickly grow on the DCI's face.

"You mean she escaped, Kinnaird? I'm surprised you didn't shoot her."

"It crossed my mind, but I knew you'd be upset."

Colin Evans was standing behind Ship, his head slowly shaking, but Ship ignored the remark. "How certain are you that Fisher is responsible for the murders?"

"He wears a red wig, strapless high heels, and uses a blade. He also has the best motive. He wants to take over the north's vice racket."

"Can you prove that?" The DCI was suddenly very interested in what Kinnaird had to say and leaned towards him, his face a mask of concentration. "I don't imagine he's the kind to plead?"

"Depends on whether we can persuade him that we've a good case. At the moment he thinks he'll be out of here in a couple of hours. Something to do with a high-level connection."

"We'll have to disappoint him," Ship replied firmly, yet sensing the best was yet to come. "Who is this high-level connection?"

Kinnaird rose to his feet and whispered Sir Alexander Hodgkiss' name into the DCI's ear. The senior detective was wide-eyed with surprise and nodded.

"Let's keep that to ourselves for the moment. I want you to interrogate Fisher. Sergeant Moran will assist you."

Kinnaird eyed Moran. They had not worked together before. The sergeant was a recent addition to the CID strength at Fulham, though he had been in the department for several years. "No offence, Bill, but I want to be the one throwing the questions at him."

Moran was in his late-thirties with a face that suggested it had experienced just about everything. He smiled. "I don't have a problem with that."

"May I also sit in?" Mowatt asked.

"Haven't you had enough for one day?" Evans asked, genuinely concerned for her welfare.

"Let her," the DCI told him. "She's earned it." To Kinnaird he said, "You can have your warrant card back, collect it from my office before you leave."

"I might be working quite late."

"I'll be there to hear how you made out with Fisher." He turned away and headed towards the exit with everyone's eyes glued to his back.

In one of the two interview rooms at Fulham police station Kinnaird sat opposite Sonny Fisher, a desk separating them. Detective Sergeant Bill Moran and Police Constable Melanie Mowatt spectated from a distance.

Fisher wore a sullen, sulky expression, like a child refused his way. "I want my brief!"

"Later! You became a major player in the south's vice racket just over a year ago, a short time after Sir Alexander Hodgkiss provided you with the financial clout you needed. He's also backing your takeover in the north."

Fisher failed to hide his surprise at mention of Hodgkiss' name. "So you know a few of my heavy-duty contacts, what of it?"

"We also know that you've been making serious moves to take over Duffy's empire. Right now you and Hodgkiss are prime suspects for several murders which seem linked to your takeover bid."

"I don't know what you're talking about. I want my brief in here now before I say another word!"

"You're finished, Sonny. I heard you discussing Duffy in the Jamaica club, and how much longer you thought it'd be before his business folded. Your only hope is to co-operate with us."

"You're not scaring me, you bastard!" A tremor in his voice said otherwise.

"Aren't I, Sonny . . . not even a little?" He paused allowing his words to immerse Fisher in a swell of apprehension. "Are you willing to pay the price alone for several murders?"

"I didn't murder anyone," his voice trembled, anxious, lonely for support.

"You had the best motive and fit our description of the killer to a tee. No court will let you walk. The evidence against you is overwhelming. But I want your partner, Hodgkiss, because this whole thing is about the two of you."

"I really didn't murder anyone. Honestly, you've got to believe me. Please!" His eyes were wide open and pleading, desperate to be believed.

Kinnaird had heard pleas from dozens of suspects claiming their innocence. Most were guilty. Belief is a complex emotion, understood through regular acquaintance or instinct borne on the wings of experience. At that moment the latter applied to Kinnaird: every fibre, every tissue in his body told him Fisher was genuine. Only his mind contradicted his instincts, laying out facts such as the strapless high heels, red wig, knife and, above all, motive. What made Fisher different? He asked himself again and again, but came up with no answer other than gut feeling, something which refused to be ignored. When he spoke his voice held no threats. "Do you have any alibis?"

"The night the attack at the hospital took place I was sleeping with Debbie Ash."

"If you're going to lie, at least try making it convincing. You come across to me as someone who prefers men. I can't imagine you with her."

"Maybe I do, but sometimes, in the dark, she can be very . . . . masculine." His expression was that of a boy recalling something special.

Kinnaird wondered, wondered why he believed Fisher even when he came out with something as outrageously ridiculous as Debbie Ash for an alibi. Yet he did. "Is she the only alibi you've got?"

"When most of the attacks occurred I was with her. She'd tell you . . . . "

"I wouldn't count on it." He pushed a statement sheet and pen in front of Fisher. "I want you to write your own statement. Put in it everything you did to take over Duffy's business, and include all you know about Hodgkiss. If what you know only amounts to him beating pros to a pulp, put it down. I want that pervert, and you're going to help me get him."

Fisher began writing almost immediately. When he had finished Kinnaird read the statement.

"What does Hodgkiss see in Debbie Ash?"

Fisher leaned away from the desk and crossed his legs. A dark stockinged knee caught Kinnaird's eye as it rose above desk level, and the detective chastised himself for noticing. "He dotes on her . . . . she knows how to please him better than anyone I know, except me."

"Is that why you've used her as a main bitch?"

"Partly, but she's good at it, and the girls trust her. She knows every trick they can work to avoid paying and they know it. She treats them fair and gets a good return for her trouble."

"Why did you pay Mona Curtis to stay away from her?"

"She's too friendly with Duffy, she'd be telling him every move I made if I'd let her stay. She and 'The Man' were quite strong at one time, I mean businesswise. She was his main bitch for almost five years, there was no one better at the job, so I've heard. Then Debbie showed up and took the black cow's mind off her work. Duffy was forced to climb back behind the steering-wheel when Mona lost interest. He didn't like it much and got himself another main bitch, but she didn't last, nor did the one after that. Then I heard only the other day that Mona was back on his payroll."

Kinnaird nodded, his eyes running over Fisher's statement at a part which included Hodgkiss. "What do you think Hodgkiss' reaction will be when he discovers that you're in bed with a bunch of druggies? Personally, I reckon you've a good chance of losing any support you might have had from that direction. It'll be political dynamite as far as he's concerned. He'll be too busy distancing himself from you, covering his back with his own supporters to care about you. You're going down, Sonny, and just maybe Hodgkiss will get away with murder, but you definitely won't."

"I've given you what you wanted, Kinnaird. I've put it down just as you asked. It's all I know he did!"

"OK." Kinnaird felt a rush of excitement pulse through his veins. Fisher had provided them with sufficient evidence to arrest Hodgkiss; obtaining more would rest with the tycoon's interrogation. Fisher could go no further.

George Ship, the DCI, was in his office when Kinnaird knocked at his door. "How far did you get with Fisher?"

"Downstairs we've a man who fits the description of our killer, and has a good motive for the murders. He also claims that he was aware Hodgkiss attacked Duffy's toms to feed his sadistic perversions, and that Hodgkiss used the name Hastings as an alias to keep his identity secret. Here's his statement."

Ship read it through, "But he doesn't admit to the murders himself. Well, as far as I'm concerned, he's going to have to prove his innocence to a court."

Kinnaird, reluctant to share his personal view, uncharacteristically refrained from doing so. He doubted Ship would listen anyway, the mood he was in; and even if he did, he wouldn't understand; he was not the type. As it wasn't written down that policemen could work on instinct, then it didn't happen. Kinnaird decided to wait until he had heard what Sir Alexander Hodgkiss had to say. "We need to talk to Hodgkiss."

"You make it sound simple, but all we've got is the word of a fairy vice king to take on one of the richest men in the country?"

"Rich he might be, but we can prove that he's also a sadist who enjoys punching the daylights out of women. Fisher's willing to bring forward all the toms Hodgkiss damaged. It's how this thing with Duffy's women began. Fisher suggested to the great man that he come over here on safari, because he was running out of toms willing to take the punishment Hodgkiss was meting out. The idea appealed so much Sir Alexander did just that, and got an extra buzz from the risks involved in attacking women on the streets, on top of that it didn't cost him a penny. All Fisher had to do from then on was keep someone in hand for Hodgkiss to perform natural sex with, if that's what you can call it."

"Debbie Ash?"

"Now you're beginning to understand how simple this really is."

"Very neat, but can we prove it?" The DCI frowned as he imagined more negative headlines, especially from Hodgkiss' newspapers.

"If we don't act on this information we'll be criticised because people are going to wonder what stopped us. When Fisher goes to court it'll come out in the open, and the public might think that Hodgkiss bought us off."

"And if you're wrong, we'll be criticised for listening to the likes of Sonny Fisher, a fairy vice king, and taking his word against such an eminent man."

"There's something else you haven't mentioned, which I'm certain you're thinking about." Kinnaird watched as the DCI's eyes narrowed. "Hodgkiss is going to be a banner headline, and because we can prove that he's a sadistic pervert, there's going to be a certain amount of glory attached to exposing what a nasty person he really is."

"You're one hell of a bullshitter, Kinnaird, but then you know that. Now just tell me how you'd handle this?" Ship's decision whether they interviewed Hodgkiss was still hovering, all Kinnaird was certain was that he would not be leading the investigation to the tycoon's front door.

"We bring him here for questioning, and leave him in a cell, that'll throw him off guard." Kinnaird was right and Ship knew it. Hodgkiss, a high-profile public figure, would consider arrest and interview at a police station demeaning. But that was only part of it, the rest was to leave him alone stewing in a cell to create a classless demoralising affect that would turn him into a willing talker. Even hardened criminals had ceded to the solitude of four stone walls as imagination and guilt teased their conscience. The police were empowered to prevent news reaching inmates for up to three days. A long time when charges might mean life imprisonment. It came as no surprise that nerves regularly broke and crimes were admitted in the hope of a reduced sentence.

"You realise what you're requesting?" Ship asked him, still undecided.

"We have reasonable suspicion, that's all it takes."

"We've the word of a fairy vice king."

"He's still a member of the public!"

"Damn it, Kinnaird, this whole thing could be a hoax to make us look bad, just like with Macaulay?"

"Someone else besides Fisher told me about Hodgkiss, and I believe him."

The DCI rose to his feet and moved to a window as a cloud crossed the face of the moon. "Tell Colin Evans I want to see him. He'll take the lead on this one, and none of you are going armed." Kinnaird turned to leave, but Ship had not finished. "Don't forget to pick up your warrant card, it's on my desk."

The detective collected his ID from the desk and looked back at the other man, "Thanks."

"Don't thank me, Kinnaird, I don't deserve it."

Sir Alexander Hodgkiss lived in a three-storey terraced house in Curzon Street, the heart of Mayfair. It was late by the time the DI, DS Moran and Kinnaird stood outside his front door and rang the bell. An unmarked police car with Mowatt behind the wheel waited for them. When the door opened an old man with greying hair and wearing a woollen dressing-gown greeted them. He was tall, very thin and did not look strong.

"Yes, gentlemen?" He was also polite, in an abrupt way.

"We'd like to see Sir Alexander," Evans told him.

"I'm afraid that's not possible, he retired to his bed just

over an hour ago," he made it sound as if everyone else should have done the same. "If you wish to leave a message, I'll see that it's received first thing in the morning."

"Tell Sir Alexander that the police want to speak to him," the DI showed the old man his ID. "Tell him it's important, and that we're not leaving until we've seen him."

"I see." For a moment he looked confused, then he stepped aside. "Perhaps you should wait in the hall."

The detectives stepped into a large hallway with a wide staircase running up to an open landing. What struck the DI as the old man trundled slowly up the stairs was the all white decor. "Reminds me of a hospital."

"Kind of grand though," Moran added.

"He painted this himself," Kinnaird read the signature on a painting of a country scene.

"When you've this much dough, you've time to learn how to paint," Evans sounded envious.

Sir Alexander Hodgkiss was an impressive-looking figure. He swept down the stairs with his eyes fixed on the DI and ignored the others. He was tall, stocky, and wore a gold satin robe that was a perfect match for his broad physique. Anyone might have been excused for believing him ten years younger than fifty, even though a shock of white hair either side of his temple went some way to betraying the truth. His expression was grave, with a strong, straight jaw a shade too tight. When he spoke there was nothing hostile about his tone, more a strong curiosity. He held out a large hand, as his soft, cultured voice used words with a precision that could not be faulted. "I understand that you wish to speak to me, Inspector, about something important?"

"Yes, sir," Evans lost the starch from his voice that he had used on the old man, and even showed a little humility in the presence of someone so distinguished. "I apologise for the lateness of the hour, but I'm certain that you'll appreciate our reasons when I tell you that we're investigating several murders."

"Gosh, I do hope that I'm not a suspect," he laughed, as if expecting the detectives to do the same, then stopped abruptly when none did. On a more serious note he said, "Perhaps we should step into the drawing- room." He led them towards a pair of tall doors with brass handles, and pushed them inwards. The detectives followed him inside as he flicked on a light. The room was all green: walls, ceiling, furniture, carpet and an elaborate chandelier. "Before you begin, Inspector, may I offer you all a drink?"

"No thank you, sir, we don't want to detain you any longer than necessary."

"Very thoughtful of you." Hodgkiss moved towards a large open fireplace with a pair of green painted lions acting as columns on either side. "Now then, what's this all about?"

"You might prefer it if we spoke in private, Sir Alexander?" Evans glanced at the old man standing in the doorway.

"Of course. Charles, that will be all for tonight. I'll see the officers out, you go back to bed."

The old man scanned the unfamiliar faces, nodded, then closed the doors behind him as he backed out.

"We understand that you're an associate of Sonny Fisher, sir." Evans didn't waste time.

"I know him. Is he responsible for these murders?" Hodgkiss sounded and appeared like a man who wanted to help.

"He was arrested this afternoon and taken to Fulham police station. He told us that you were a business partner."

"Business partner!" Hodgkiss chuckled, "Hardly! He's a greengrocer, isn't he?"

"Well I've heard what he does referred to by many names, but never that." The DI spotted a mask of confusion appear on Hodgkiss' brow. "Sonny Fisher runs the largest vice racket south of the Thames."

"I had no idea." Hodgkiss expressed surprise that the detectives could only wonder at. "We're not really friends, acquaintances is a more apt word. We met on several social occasions, but I never pushed to find out much about him. I heard that he owned a grocery chain."

"Fisher has suggested that your relationship is more intimate."

"Has he?" Hodgkiss held the DI's gaze for a moment. "There are other witnesses who agree," Evans sensed him waver, a second of uncertainty that would not have been there if Fisher had lied. The DI was thinking of the information supplied by Duffy, unusable in a courtroom, but Hodgkiss was not to know. "I realise this must be very difficult for you, Sir Alexander . . . . "

"Embarrassing I'm afraid, but I can see that there is little point in my lying; that to do so will only make matters worse. I am bisexual, very few people know that. Sonny Fisher and I had an affair, but that finished some time ago."

"That's not what Fisher has told us . . . . "

"I don't give a damn what he told you!" Hodgkiss snapped and looked immediately sorry. "I apologise, Inspector, but Sonny Fisher was a great mistake on my part, something I regret and have been attempting to forget. I hope that I'm not to be persecuted because of my folly."

"He refers to you as a financial backer for his criminal activities. More seriously, he alleges that you've been attacking prostitutes in the Fulham area, assisting him in a takeover bid for the largest vice racket north of the Thames."

"But that's absurd. I don't require money from criminal activities, I'm a millionaire several times over. I own a couple of Fleet Street newspapers and all kinds of legitimate businesses. Why should I get involved in such sordid shenanigans? More shocking is that a criminal has given you my name, and you're willing to act on his ridiculous allegations. I find that most disturbing!"

"Fisher found out about your sadistic streak and supplied you with prostitutes who were willing to be beaten."

"I don't wish to hear anymore . . . . "

"You have no choice, sir," Evans insisted. "I told you this is a murder enquiry, therefore we can either discuss the matter here or at Fulham police station."

"Perhaps I should contact my lawyer?"

"Certainly, if you've something to hide."

Hodgkiss glared at Evans as their gazes momentarily locked in silent combat. "As that is not the case, I shall allow you to have your say, Inspector, but please be succinct. I need to rise early tomorrow."

"Before I continue, I should again like to point out that we are not here solely on the word of Sonny Fisher." The DI allowed a moment for his words to register, then proceeded with a matter-of-fact delivery. "After a time Fisher's prostitutes stopped coming to you, because they found you too violent. Fisher then had the idea of you attacking Duffy's women. He saw it as killing two birds with one stone: you fed your twisted habit while his competitor was being put out of business because his women were too scared to work."

"You make it sound as if you've already made up your mind about me, but the whole thing is quite preposterous, and should word of it leak out I will hold you personally responsible. I may sue the Met for every penny it's got, and by the end of it you'll be looking for a new line of employment!"

The threat sparked something in Evans that showed in the way he narrowed his eyes. "I want to know your whereabouts on the night of the fifth of December."

"How should I know? I can't be expected to remember something like that straight off the top of my head!"

"I suggest you try . . . . sir. Otherwise you'll leave us no alternative but to continue this enquiry in a police cell." Hodgkiss stared at him, speechless for a moment. "You must keep a diary, we'll wait here while you fetch it."

"Yes, of course . . . . it's upstairs in my bedroom." He turned to leave.

"Go with him, Del."

Hodgkiss rounded on them, "Am I to be treated as a petty criminal in my own home, for God's sake?"

"I'd hardly call murder petty, but until you've cleared yourself I want to be certain that you don't go missing."

"I don't like your manner, Inspector, and I'll be saying as much to your seniors!"

"That's your privilege, Sir Alexander."

Hodgkiss went to his bedroom with Kinnaird acting as escort. As with downstairs, the bedroom was painted a single colour, blue. Parked against a wall a tall glass cabinet housed several trophies; on a low shelf were miniature statuettes of boxers in defensive postures. Kinnaird noted them as he followed Hodgkiss to a bedside drawer and watched it being pulled open. The black butt of a pistol was the first thing he saw, and he reacted automatically, slamming the drawer shut on the other man's hand. Hodgkiss yelped and jumped back.

"What on earth did you do that for?"

"I'm allergic to lead." The detective reopened the drawer and relieved it of a small .32 pistol.

184

"My diary was under it," Hodgkiss rubbed his tender fingers, his earlier composure only a memory in the detective's mind. "I have a licence for that."

"Do you have any other weapons, say a large hunting knife?"

"If I go hunting I do so with a rifle, not a knife."

Kinnaird found it easy to imagine Hodgkiss liked doing things at a distance. Being any good as a boxer meant that you had to keep opponents at a distance, otherwise you got hurt. Shooting was the same, except further. Using a knife was the opposite, no distance at all, provided you didn't throw it. Most knife men kept them firmly in hand because you only got one chance if you didn't. "If you've a licence for this thing, the local police would wish you to keep it in a safer place than a bedside drawer."

"Someone like you may not have the capacity to appreciate the value of the paintings around you." Hodgkiss exhibited a brand of contempt which proved he gave little credit to those with a more humble income. It had no affect on Kinnaird, partly because the detective would soon assist in removing the tycoon from his grand house in a manner no better than a petty criminal. He listened further as Hodgkiss continued in the same tone. "I own many highly prized art treasures, that's why I keep this gun close to hand. Should I store it where your people recommended, it would be of no use whatsoever should a burglar break in."

Kinnaird cleared his throat, then said, "You may not have the capacity to appreciate this, but you're not meant to shoot burglars. The diary can wait. Where's the licence?"

"In the wardrobe." He nodded towards a huge fitted cabinet, the kind a person could walk around, with clothes hanging on either side of a narrow aisle. At one end of the aisle was a full-length mirror. Hodgkiss moved to the wardobe with a reluctant gait and stopped by its door. "Is this really necessary?"

"Humour me." Kinnaird watched from the doorway as he kneeled down on the aisle floor and pulled back a fitted carpet. Under it was a small safe protected by a combination lock. Hodgkiss blocked Kinnaird's view of what he was doing with a shoulder. When he unscrambled the combination and pulled open the safe door, he quickly found the licence and closed the safe, scrambling the lock.

"Here it is." He handed Kinnaird the licence and moved away from the wardrobe as if he wanted to put some distance between it and them. "Now, shall we take a look in my diary so that I may clear myself?"

Hodgkiss stood alongside the bedside drawer and flicked through the diary. "I was at home on the night of December fifth."

"Was anyone with you?"

"My butler. He'll be able to confirm that I was here. No, he won't, he took some leave early in December and didn't return until the tenth."

"So what you're saying is that you don't have an alibi for the fifth of December?"

"I'm sure I'm not the only person in this country who cannot provide an alibi for that date."

"But you're the only one we're interested in. When did you last see Debbie Ash?"

His expression suddenly changed to a picture of troubled understanding. "So she's involved, I should have guessed. No wonder you're so confident."

"We'd hardly have come here with just the word of a fairy vice king," Kinnaird sensed an opening, Debbie Ash the key. Hodgkiss turned pale, suddenly jaded behind a mask of painful resignation, his shoulders slumped forward, and his strong jaw lost its defiance. It happened so quickly Kinnaird wondered if he were ill.

"I suppose that it was only a matter of time before something like this happened. I heard that you'd arrested Mona Curtis. I suppose that you've been playing with me?"

"We wanted to hear what you'd say." Kinnaird leaned against a wall as if he had all the time in the world. "But now that you know what you're up against, I'd be willing to listen to your side of the story. I'm certain you'll point out discrepancies with their version."

"I was being blackmailed. They . . . . " He moved away, pacing the bedroom carpet, as if it helped get his thinking straight.

"That's how Fisher kept you as a banker?"

Hodgkiss stopped and stared at the detective, his face suddenly flushed, his eyes angry. "You tricked me!"

"I did?" Kinnaird frowned, the question a mistake. Somehow it put Hodgkiss on the defensive, but the detective was uncertain why.

"You know damn well you did! I think that I should call my lawyer before I say anything more."

"You can do that from the station, Sir Alexander." Evans spoke from the doorway as he and Moran stepped into the bedroom.

"Am I under arrest?"

"Yes, sir, for murder."

"I haven't murdered anyone, but I have been blackmailed." Hodgkiss strode towards the DI determined to be taken seriously as a victim.

"Who blackmailed you?" Evans remained impassive, distant.

"I . . . . I can't say . . . . not, not without first discussing my position with my lawyer."

"Suit yourself, you can talk to him in three days' time after we've had a chance to dig around a little more. Unless you decide that you can't face the prospect of living in a cell for that long?"

"You can't stop me from calling my . . . . "

"That's precisely what I can do!" Evans growled. "If I believe this investigation will be hampered by your contact with anyone, including your lawyer!"

"You're treading on thin ice Inspector, my newspapers will . . . . '

"Do nothing," the DI snapped, growing angrier with every threat Hodgkiss raised. "You're a murder suspect, that's what we'll be telling your newspapers. Your competitors, on the other hand, are likely to report the fact that you're also a pervert."

Hodgkiss faltered, perhaps wishing that he had more time to think, to invent a story or even tell the truth, but he wanted advice, needed it, and even that was being deprived him. His clear blue eyes busily searched the faces of the detectives, probing for an escape route to avoid his imminent incarceration. "Inspector, you must forgive me, I'm naturally upset by all of this, couldn't we discuss the matter like reasonable men?"

"What did you have in mind?" Evans replied, his tone restrained.

"Let's see, there are three of you, but of course rank has its privileges. Let's say ten thousand for each of your men and twenty thousand for yourself."

"You really do appear to understand the gravity of your situation, Sir Alexander." The other detectives looked at the

DI, but neither spoke.

"I'm afraid that I didn't do that quickly enough, but you have helped me." Hodgkiss turned back towards the wardrobe. "I have the money in my safe."

"I'm glad, we don't take cheques," Evans nodded for Kinnaird to follow him.

When Hodgkiss opened the safe the detective looked over his shoulder to check for more weapons, but the safe was so crammed full of twenty pound notes there was no room. Kinnaird let out a low whistle.

"It's my slush fund," Hodgkiss explained.

"Tax paid of course?"

"What the taxman doesn't see won't hurt him."

"How much has he got, Del?" Evans asked from the doorway.

"Haven't a clue, Colin. I've never seen this much money before."

Hodgkiss looked over his shoulder at the DI, "Let's make it fifty thousand for you, Inspector, and twenty-five each for your men."

"Very generous, Sir Alexander, but I want it all out here on the bed."

"But, but you can't . . . . we had an understanding!" Hodgkiss rose to his feet clutching a bundle of twenties to his chest.

"Wrong. You just attempted a bribe. We said no!"

"But . . . . but," he spluttered with confusion.

"Put it all on the bed. Del, make certain nothing is left behind."

"You have no right to do this!"

"You're a murder suspect, and you just attempted to bribe us with illegal money. We have the right. On top of that

I'm sure the Inland Revenue are going to be very interested to know how you came by that stash."

When the money had been piled on the bed, Kinnaird returned to the safe then re-emerged from the wardrobe with a handful of photographs and a couple of magazines. The photographs showed Hodgkiss, naked except for a pair of boxing gloves. His companions were Sheenarena and Tina Wilson. Both women were black and blue from beatings, while only their faces had not been touched. Hodgkiss shook his head and slumped down on the bed, crushed. "They blackmailed me. I didn't murder anyone. I want my lawyer."

"You'll need him!" The DI turned to Moran. "I want that money counted in front of Sir Alexander, there must be no suggestion later on that it was not all accounted for." To Hodgkiss he said, "Get dressed, you're coming back to the station with us."

Hodgkiss was placed in a cell at Fulham police station and told that he would be interviewed in the morning. The detectives then collected in the charge room, Evans looking pleased with himself.

"Looks like we've cracked it! Those photographs of Hodgkiss beating the dead toms convinced me that we've got him by the short and curlies!"

"It's very neat," Kinnaird muttered just loud enough to be heard.

"You have a problem with neat?" The DI's exuberance wavered.

"He told us that he was being blackmailed. Perhaps we should have asked him who the blackmailers are?"

"That's Fisher, he probably took the pictures of Hodgkiss beating a couple of our victims." Evans looked at Moran and Mowatt for agreement, but they were watching Kinnaird.

"None of the girls were actually dead in any of the photographs."

"They'd been beaten, that's good enough for me. I don't see why you're not satisfied, you're the one who wanted Hodgkiss nicked . . . . Sonny Fisher is the obvious blackmailer."

"Maybe, but Hodgkiss referred to the blackmailers as them, more than one person." He glanced at their faces in turn as if checking they understood what he was driving at. "Anyone who controls Hodgkiss also has access to his enormous wealth . . . . And now I'm not one hundred per cent certain that was Fisher alone."

"Maybe you're being too clever, Del." The DI stifled a yawn with his hand. "Anyway, I don't think the blackmail business is important. What is, is that we've caught the killers. The rest can wait till the morning, they aren't going anywhere. Be here at nine sharp, I want to get started nice and early."

No one argued. Kinnaird gave Mowatt a lift to her police accommodation, expecting her to be full of questions about what had happened in the house with Hodgkiss, but she remained quiet during the journey. He pulled up outside the grey stone section house and waited for her to climb out, but she didn't move.

"Are you all right, Mel?"

"Thanks for everything, Del," her voice was a soft purr.

"It was only a ten-minute drive."

"That's not what I meant." She turned to him, her eyes emotional, enquiring. "We've done some exciting things together. I don't think it could have happened with anyone else. You've been . . . . ' she stopped as if searching for the right words. "You saved my life and took a lot of personal

191

risks, and I must seem ungrateful because I hardly mentioned what you'd done . . . . "

"I'd have done the same for any colleague." He felt suddenly uncomfortable, for both of them. "Forget it, you can do the same for me one day."

"I'll never forget it."

"Are you sure that you're OK?"

She moved so that the darkness shrouded her face and prevented him seeing the answer in her eyes. "I'd like to say more, but I don't want you to get the wrong idea."

"Sounds serious. If it's any help I haven't had a wrong idea in hours."

"It's just that I want you to know . . . . " she stumbled for the words, then blurted them out. "I understand why a lot of people admire you."

"They do?"

She shifted, turning towards him, their mouths suddenly close. He breathed in, saw her lips part, sensed the invitation. A confused moment hovered in the air, then slipped away. "Thanks, Del."

She climbed out of the car and headed towards the section house without looking back. Kinnaird waited until she had disappeared inside, took a deep breath, and wondered if his imagination were running wild or whether Mowatt had really wanted him to kiss her.

EIGHT

In the morning Kinnaird was forty minutes late. He spotted Mowatt in the DI's office, deep in discussion. Before joining them he stopped alongside the CID clerk, Dick Clements, moved his white queen on the chessboard, and put Clements in check. The clerk growled as the detective left to join the others.

"I was worried the afternoon was going to get here before you." Evans could always be counted on to make a point.

"Sorry." Kinnaird glanced at Mowatt who did not look up. There was a sense of embarrassment about her that only he noticed, a hangover from the night before. It confirmed that it hadn't simply been his imagination working overtime.

"Bill Moran is at court this morning so the three of us will be interrogating Hodgkiss." The DI appeared to miss that Mowatt avoided eye-contact with Kinnaird. "I spoke to the station officer who took our distinguished guest some breakfast, and says that he doesn't think cell life agrees with him. There's a good chance he'll be willing to cough."

"How's George Ship bearing up under the strain of having someone as powerful as Hodgkiss in one of his cells?"

"He's just thankful that you didn't kill anyone last night. He thinks it's a definite improvement in your overall approach."

"Is there any other incoming flak, apart from what you're throwing at me?"

"For the moment it's survivable. Hodgkiss has a lawyer who's doing the rounds, but we're stalling. When the lid finally lifts it's going to be the press we'll be struggling with." The DI rose to his feet. "By the way, I slept on your questions over the blackmail, and came up with a few questions of my own. The first being, was Hodgkiss really blackmailed? There's reason to doubt it, after all it's a good defence. If he were, then Fisher had the opportunity and resources to get Hodgkiss nailed to a wall, and is the type to do it. He may have had help, of course, hence Hodgkiss referring to a couple of blackmailers. I expect Debbie Ash put in some effort to get him compromised, but that's all I imagine happened. I want this wrapped up so they both go down . . . Fisher's the killer and we'll get Hodgkiss for aiding and abetting. That, by the way, also fits in with your theory that the puncher wouldn't have used a blade. Besides, I think it's the best we'll get for the big man, that's how I see it."

Kinnaird nodded. He had also spent time thinking about who might have blackmailed Hodgkiss, except what he came up with didn't agree with Evans. It was a wild idea anyway but maybe it was possible. Debbie Ash was the key, and she worked for Duffy. The vice king was a master, a legend in his lifetime, and perhaps he had orchestrated the attacks on his own people to bring about Fisher's destruction. There was no doubt Fisher was finished, while Hodgkiss would only want to disassociate himself from the transvestite, leaving the south vice rackets wide open. Duffy had known about Hodgkiss and perhaps through Debbie Ash had blackmailed him to support his strategy against Fisher. Kinnaird was still playing with the idea, but it was growing on him. "I'd like to go find Debbie Ash. If for no other reason than because Fisher's using her as an alibi."

"Let's go talk to the big man first." The DI led the way with Kinnaird while Mowatt trailed behind, far enough not to be included in their conversation, but close enough for it not to be obvious.

When they opened the cell door, Hodgkiss stood with his arms folded, a pasty, sullen shell of his former self. Overnight he appeared to have aged ten years. Lines around his red-rimmed eyes showed that sleep had been elusive, while a growth of stubble occupied his chin, probably the longest it had ever been. He ran his fingers through his hair in an attempt to make it tidy, but with little effect. The DI and Kinnaird stood in front of him while Mowatt made herself comfortable on a bench, a notebook on her lap.

"We'd like to hear about the blackmailers," Evans began.

"Then you believe that I'm not a murderer?"

"That's not what I said. We still need convincing, if we've doubts before today's over, you'll be charged. So start talking!"

Hodgkiss shook his head and sighed before joining Mowatt on the bench. "I'll only admit that I'm bisexual – nothing more." Evans' face reddened angrily, "We're going round the bloody mulberry bush. What about the women you paid to let you beat them?"

"I paid them well, and they were still alive when I'd finished."

"So who killed them?" The DI dug his hands into his trouser pockets and loomed over the other man, his foot tapping noisily against the tiled floor as he waited for an answer.

"Why don't you tell me who you think killed them?" Hodgkiss replied defiantly. His night spent without sleep had been used constructively, planning a strategy, in the same way he might a business deal. What was obvious was that he had decided to keep his co-operation limited.

"I thought we were getting somewhere," Evans replied irritably. "But it looks like we'll have to do this the hard way."

"I didn't murder anyone, Inspector. I paid for my fetish, and the girls were always alive when I left them. I have nothing more to add." Hodgkiss was wriggling, searching for a gap in the net closing around him, gauging the detectives' reactions, sensing his way through a minefield of police tactics. The detectives had underestimated him, relying on a night's confinement as sufficient to push him over the edge, but it hadn't worked. He spotted the dour expression on Mowatt's face and grew an understanding smile, "Do you think me a beast?"

"I think you need help," she replied.

"I knew that you wouldn't understand." He sounded distant, and looked away, as if recalling something in the past. "Sonny and Debbie both understood."

"Unless you help us identify the killer, you're going to be charged with complicity." Evans threatened.

"I want to speak to my lawyer. I've nothing more to say to you."

"Who's been blackmailing you?" Kinnaird asked, but the other man simply shook his head. "Was it Debbie Ash?"

"You used the name Hastings to keep your identity secret, we can prove that." Evans began to pace the floor.

"I wouldn't deny it. My motives weren't unreasonable."

"Did you go with Fisher to the hospital and murder all those people?"

"I keep telling you, I haven't murdered anyone. I want to speak to my lawyer."

"You're going to spend the next three days in this cell, Hodgkiss, without seeing anyone except us. In that time if you don't make a statement handing us the killer, you'll be charged. At court we'll oppose bail so you might as well get used to this environment. This is one time your money isn't going to bail you out!"

When they left Hodgkiss, Kinnaird was even keener to find Debbie Ash. "That little minx could be the key that makes Fisher and Hodgkiss open up."

"Maybe," Evans shrugged, "but where will you find her?"

"She's working for Duffy, Fisher never knew. I expect her to go to the restaurant once she hears Hodgkiss is nicked."

Evans looked suddenly anxious. "I don't want anyone hurt, Del, including you or Mel. If you spot her outside the restaurant, pick her up but don't go inside and tackle her alone, call for support. Duffy might take umbrage otherwise."

"Sure." Kinnaird wondered how Duffy felt about his reneging on their deal by not killing Fisher. Not that he gave a damn, especially now Vienna was out of reach. They were enemies, could never be anything else. No one other than Mowatt knew about their broken agreement, and he could rely on her not to mention it. Yet to catch Debbie Ash and avoid a confrontation with Duffy would not be easy.

"Sound a little more reassuring will you? You stick outside Duffy's place and observe, no more or less. I'll have a few others pay Ash's aunt a visit, she may have gone there." The DI glanced at Mowatt. "Keep a tight leash on him, Mel!"

As they stepped through the exit, Kinnaird threw her the car keys, "You drive."

"How come?" she asked, surprised, events outside the

section house the previous night temporarily shelved.

Kinnaird pulled out a .32 pistol as he climbed into the car. "I need to check this. I found it at Hodgkiss' house last night and forgot to hand it in."

"Why didn't you simply ask Evans to go armed?"

"Because he would have said no."

"I won't be a party to murder, Del." A nervous tremor in Mowatt's voice caught his attention. He returned the pistol to his pocket.

"I'm no murderer, but we may need this."

"Duffy might try making good his threat – is that what you're hoping? You hate each other and this might be the opportunity to settle it."

Kinnaird listened to her without interruption. That she was wrong didn't matter, what did was that she thought she was right. She really believed he wanted to kill Duffy. Vienna would have known better, but then Mowatt wasn't Vienna. "We're going to arrest Debbie Ash, that's all. If Duffy gets in the way he gets arrested too. Now get this thing started or do you want me to drive?"

Mowatt parked in a side street facing the restaurant's main entrance. "There's only one thing wrong with waiting here as far as I can see," she glanced at Kinnaird. "Debbie might already be inside."

"Too early, it's only eleven thirty. I doubt she's an early riser, so she won't have heard about Hodgkiss yet."

"One of us should go in there for a meal, that way we also cover the back door without freezing to death."

"Feeling hungry?"

"You know it makes sense."

"And you know I can't, so I guess you're volunteering?"

"Duffy only saw me once, and it wasn't for long."

"Don't underrate yourself. He took a good look at you and never forgets a body." He did not like what she had in mind, even if it did make sense. Yet he tried to remain objective, to pretend that she was just like a male colleague. It was very, very hard. "If anything were to happen to you, George Ship would have my head."

"Don't use him as an excuse, Kinnaird. You know it doesn't matter what anyone else says or does. You're worried about me yourself, why don't you admit it?" She began tying her hair in a bun then searched through her handbag and dug out a pair of spectacles. Kinnaird looked surprised when she put them on, "They're not real, it's ordinary glass, but I keep them for just such occasions."

"And Colin Evans wanted you to keep me on a short leash!" He shook his head, and conceded that she did look a little different. "OK, if you have to hear it . . . . I'd worry about you being in there alone, but don't get any wrong ideas."

"I haven't had one of those since last night," she giggled. "But don't worry, I can tell when someone's unavailable. It was sweet of you not to take advantage of me in my moment of weakness. I thank you for that."

"I can't deny that I wasn't tempted." He leaned back on the seat and stared at the restaurant. "I don't want you going in there too early, wait until they're busy."

"Would you mind if I did a little shopping first? I need a new umbrella and spotted some for sale just around the corner." Kinnaird shrugged. "Remember to wait until the place fills up."

She climbed out of the car and strode towards the Fulham Road. Kinnaird noted that the jeans she wore did nothing to detract from her femininity, then she rounded a corner and disappeared. He switched on the car radio and listened to a depressed-sounding weatherman report that freezing temperatures would continue for the foreseeable future. It did not come as a surprise. He thumbed the frequency dial and found a news programme reviewing the Cod War won by Iceland in June. The detective switched off the radio wondering why he had even bothered, the news never seemed good these days.

A heavy rain was falling by the time Mowatt reappeared, half-hidden beneath a large yellow umbrella. Kinnaird groaned at the conspicuous colour, and again when she stepped into the restaurant without first checking whether it had filled up. Not for the first time he wished Wright were with him, there would have been less reason for him to worry. But it would be a few more weeks before his friend was back.

Time dragged, the weather remained freezing, and hailstones fell while Kinnaird watched people come and go. By three in the afternoon the hailstones had turned back into rain, and an unceasing downpour. He kept flicking the wiper blades across the screen to keep it clear, noting fewer people were leaving the restaurant. By four the severity of a gale force wind seemed to strengthen his own concerns for Mowatt's safety. He tried contacting the station by radio, but the hostile weather was interfering with that too, a crackle of unintelligible static replied to his message. He climbed out of the car and met the wind and rain head on. At the restaurant entrance, as the elements lashed him with growing fury, he found the doors locked from the inside. His concern for Mowatt sent a sudden chill down his spine that even the icy weather couldn't match. He raced around the building to the rear carpark, and found an unlocked door.

An empty, brightly lit kitchen stood before him, the rain making a pool around his feet as it dripped off his coat and matted hair. He moved quickly through the kitchen into the dining area and stopped, his eyes blinking to focus as they acclimatised to a fresh darkness created by dimmer switch lighting turned low. As soon as his vision returned he began to search, but there was no one. A door labelled Private sat behind a small bar. With the pistol snug in his large hand he pulled the door open and was confronted by a narrow stairway that ran up to a short landing with a couple of doors facing out. He climbed the stairs two at a time, paused briefly on the landing, then opened the door to his left. Inside, he found Duffy, his arm in a sling, wearing sunglasses as he sat behind a huge oak desk. Kinnaird went to ask him about the glasses when a dozen, dazzling beams made the world disappear.

"Glad you could make it, Kinnaird." Duffy sounded amused, yet a distinctive nastiness in his tone held menace. "I guessed you wouldn't be far behind your partner."

The beams went out leaving the detective with a million multi-coloured dots blinding his vision. Before he had a chance to move, something hard and unfriendly poked him between the shoulder-blades.

"I'll take the gun," a familiar high-pitched tone echoed behind him as the pistol was pulled from his hand.

When Kinnaird's vision cleared he saw the two men Duffy had sent to Croydon standing on either side of him. Duffy had removed the sunglasses, and puffed on a cigarette. "What's the idea?"

"We're gonna have a party Kinnaird, and you'll be the star performer," he nodded to the right. On a large sofa bed Mowatt, Mona Curtis and Debbie Ash sat naked. Mowatt the only one appearing embarrassed. "You were right about my trusting Debbie too much. She and that black bitch tried to stick a blade in my heart." He nodded to his arm hanging in a sling. "If it wasn't for your girlfriend, they might've got me. My boys spotted Melanie sitting at one of the tables, and brought her up just as these two made their move. Caught 'em just in time." He turned to the prostitutes. "They came real close, closer than anyone else to wasting me."

"You want us to take them down to the station?" Kinnaird joked, guessing that was the last thing on his mind. Duffy was renowed for his ruthlessness with adversaries. It was the reason, after so many years, he was still king. Meanwhile, the detective felt more confused than ever. He had speculated that Duffy was behind the attacks against his own girls as a complex plan to rid himself of Fisher. Debbie Ash and Mona Curtis had been important components in his plan, nothing more. So why had they attempted to kill him?

"You let me down by not wasting Fisher as we agreed," Duffy brought the detective back from his thoughts. "And I don't like being let down."

"Sue me."

"Oh I'm gonna do better than that. You're a dead man, Kinnaird. You've hassled me plenty over the years, now it's my turn to hand out the shit. The way I look at it, you've presented me with a golden opportunity to commit the perfect crime."

"What're you up to?" Kinnaird stepped towards him but the gun poking his back dug deeper.

Duffy laughed, "You're not as good a detective as you think. If you were you'd have known these two wanted me dead. Though it doesn't matter now, I'm clearing the rubbish out of my life, just like a spring clean. All my enemies, including you, are gonna either be dead or locked away for life."

"I don't get it. What did Debbie have to gain by murdering you?" He glanced at the blonde, trying to guess her motive. She had helped him stop Fisher and was due a fat cheque. Now, she and Curtis were meant to go off together to live happily ever after. Beside her Curtis shifted uneasily, a cornered panther with nowhere to run.

"Goes to show you just can't trust anyone in this business, especially whores. It don't matter though, not for you. Now we'll have our party – the blue movie kind, and you're gonna be the lucky stud."

"You reckon," Kinnaird sneered.

"Yeah, 'cos if you don't do as you're told my boys are gonna cut off your girlfriend's toes. If that doesn't convince you, then they'll start on her fingers. Who knows where it might end?" Duffy laughed so loud it came out like a clap of thunder.

Kinnaird glanced at Mowatt but her expression said little, other than that she was unimpressed with the naked routine. A vast mattress had been spread out in front of her, just for the occasion. She ignored it, as if what Duffy had in mind could never happen. Outside, a bellow of thunder shook the building and almost shattered a sliding glass door that led out on to a small balcony behind Duffy.

"You don't have an option, Kinnaird!" Duffy lit another cigarette and jammed it between his lips.

"After you've made your movie you'll kill us?"

"That's right," he grinned. "I want the movie for posterity. When this is over the boys are gonna take you down to an empty place I own, not too far from here, and you're gonna fry." He leaned forward with growing excitement. "There's gonna be a gas leak, then an explosion, and you'll die."

"Very imaginative, except people are going to wonder

why the four of us were there, in one of your properties."

"This is the best bit," he chuckled, smugly confident. "You came here looking for Debbie and, when I told you where you could find her, you went straight there."

"If we're going to die anyway I'm not about to perform. You cut anything off anyone, it'll show up at the autopsy."

"You're not listening, Kinnaird. The whole place is gonna go up with a bang. There'll be so many pieces of you flying around even an autopsy won't be able to match 'em up! If anyone gets suspicious, what're they gonna be able to prove other than that you died in an explosion?"

"So what's the big deal about this movie?"

"Are you kidding? Like I said, this is gonna be a perfect crime. I'll have a film of you which will comfort me when I'm feeling low."

"Well I for one won't do it!" Mowatt jumped to her feet, her knees tight together, her hands covering her breasts.

"You'll do it, kid. We got you stripped for action, didn't we?"

"Making me a porno queen won't be as easy!"

"You know what, it might be more fun if you struggle." He leaned back on the chair. "How about it girls? D'you think you can force her to spread 'em on the mattress?"

"She's right." Curtis joined Mowatt on her feet. "Why should any of us do anything if you're going to kill us anyway?"

Duffy opened a drawer and lifted out a large Bolex cine camera. "Before Debbie showed up, you were the best main bitch I ever had, Mona. We used to talk the same language. OK, you've messed up lately, but if I got rid of Debbie, maybe things could return to the way they were. Give me a performance to remember, and I'll consider letting you live."

"You're lying!" Ash jumped up. "Don't trust him, Mona!"

204

"Out of the four, Mona, you're the only one who could get through this. Are you willing to throw the chance I'm offering you away without even trying?"

"What about Debbie? Can't you just let her go?"

"Forget it, Debbie dies!" He put the camera down on the desk and gave her a chance to consider. "I reckon it was Debbie's idea to waste me, else I wouldn't even be discussing this with you."

"Some chance," Ash reached out and gripped Curtis' arm. "I won't perform for that bastard, Mona . . . . "

"You will unless you wanna die blind." The frost in Duffy's voice stoked her nerves with icy scoops of terror. She shuddered, fearful, her argument lost. "We seem to understand one another. Now, why don't you girls drag Miss Piggy on to the mattress and have some fun."

Reluctantly the women turned towards Mowatt, but still made no move to grab her. The officer shook her head, "Don't do it."

"OK boys, take out one of Debbie's eyeballs," Duffy raised the camera to his eye, anticipating their response.

The blonde pushed Mowatt on to the mattress, and the black woman twisted an arm up her back. The officer yelped, stamped a heel on Curtis' toe and pulled free. She whipped round towards Ash, the side of her foot rising swiftly, smacking hard as it met soft, white flesh. Ash flew backwards, landing on her buttocks with a thump. Behind Mowatt, the black woman loomed and punched her kidneys. She gasped, instantly breathless. Her legs buckled and she fell on to her knees.

Duffy rose to his feet, the camera against his eye as he moved to the beams that had blinded Kinnaird, readjusting them to shine on the women. When satisfied he returned to his seat behind the desk. His men moved forward for a better look. Both held guns in their hands, and Kinnaird guessed that he would be dead long before he could reach Duffy's throat. Duffy shouted at him without taking his eye from the camera, "Get your clothes off and die happy, all three are lookers."

The physical attributes of all three women made the thought of dying no easier to bear. "I don't suppose you've a condom handy?"

Duffy's surprise quickly turned to ridicule. "D'you hear that fellas? He's worried about catching something!"

"I'll take that as a no!"

"You'll enjoy it more bareback. Besides, you won't be around long enough to die from any disease, that's a promise!"

"Fortunately I'm not as confident as you about my death and don't want to take anything nasty home."

"That's right, you've got Vienna at home. She's growing up into a nice-looking piece, but don't worry about her. I'll see to it that she's comforted after you're dead." Duffy enjoyed the spectacle of anger lighting up Kinnaird's eyes. "Of course you could always plead for her. I could catch that on film, it'd be great, go on Kinnaird, plead!"

The detective spat and hit the camera lens dead centre, then someone punched the back of his head and put him down on his knees.

"Get your clothes off," Duffy snarled, taking out a cloth from the drawer and wiping the lens.

He stared up at Duffy while clutching the desk. "One thing before I do."

"You're in no position to dictate terms."

"I don't want either of your goons joining in the activity. I'll take the girls on single-handed so that you can see what it's like to be a real man."

"I always figured you had to have something special to keep Vienna. I heard she likes plenty of dick." Duffy relished taunting him, seeing every word strike home. "You really don't deserve any favours after what you just did, but then I'm a generous bloke. Bill, you and Tony keep out of it, the man thinks he's a stallion."

The expressions of his men showed their disappointment. Sex required little thought, simply animal instinct, and both looked as if they possessed plenty of that. A frenzied scream from Mowatt caught everyone's attention. Fighting on her back across the mattress, she struggled with Curtis who sprawled across her top half while Debbie Ash burrowed her head between her thighs. Frantically she grabbed the black woman's hair, but a fist hit her stomach and all at once the struggle was over.

"That's it Mona, you teach her," Duffy laughed while filming. Kinnaird slipped off his coat and jacket and let them drop to the floor in front of the bald gunman to his right. His shirt and tie followed, and covered the man's shoes. Then a low, menacing growl made the detective look up, but the sound had not been directed at him. The gunman was staring at Mona Curtis as she kneeled forward on her knees, her voluptuous rump high in the air. The detective nudged him, "I'll tell you about it."

A deep, hostile frown wrinkled the bald man's fleshy face. Kinnaird ignored it, pulled his belt free from his trousers, then dropped it with the rest of his clothes on the man's shoes. As he slipped off a brogue, Mowatt regained some of her strength and thrust Mona Curtis away. The black woman did a backwards roll and landed on hands and knees against the front of Duffy's desk, directly in front of Kinnaird and the two gunmen. The bald one stared down with wide, lustful eyes as her fleshy buttocks jiggled provocatively, then bellowed and grabbed her. As he did so, Kinnaird whacked his ear with the heel of a shoe. The gunman fell forward across the prostitute's back.

Kinnaird swung at the second gunman, smacking the weapon out of his hand. As it bounced against the floor a round banged out, loud and deafening. Kinnaird was too busy to notice, ducking a telegraphed left hook then countering with an uppercut that slammed his opponent against a door. The gunman sank to the floor almost out. Kinnaird spun round expectantly, but the other one still lay on top of Curtis, pinning her to the floor, a crimson trickle oozing from a hole at the side of his head, the only indication of where the bullet from his partner's gun had lodged. For a moment Kinnaird thought it was over. Then a sudden blow across the back of his neck put him on the floor, and somewhere in the distance, a million miles from oblivion, a woman screamed.

Kinnaird woke beneath the warm, dazzling gaze of spotlights. He pushed himself up from the floor and groaned with the effort.

"Thank God you're alive!" Mowatt shrieked. The room was empty except for her and Debbie Ash, both still naked. In one hand she held the blonde, in the other a gun.

"What happened?" Kinnaird staggered towards them, an all too familiar ache attacking the base of his skull.

"I grabbed the gun off the floor while you were keeping everyone busy. After Duffy knocked you out, I grabbed Debbie, but couldn't stop the others leaving."

"How come Mona left her behind?"

"Debbie convinced her. I was scared enough to shoot if

anyone got too close, and this little cow would've been the first to get it."

"So you let Mona walk away?" Kinnaird's tone sounded accusing, and Mowatt snapped on a frown.

"Yes, I'm sorry, but I can't shoot anyone in cold blood."

"How long have they been gone?"

"Ten minutes max. They locked the door behind them and pulled the wire out of the phone. I intended getting dressed, but this one kept me busy."

"I prefer the suit you're wearing," he grinned and plucked his shirt from the clothes on the floor.

"This is not the time, Kinnaird. Why don't you just work on getting us out of here?"

He slipped on the shirt and went across to the door. It was wooden, and thin enough to be kicked out of the way. Yet he needed to be certain no suprises were waiting on the otherside. He knelt down to peer through the key hole and caught a whiff of something rising from the gap under the door. He sniffed the air and rose quickly to his feet, "Gas!"

"You mean they're trying to blow us up in here?" Mowatt sounded like it was impossible.

"Seems they've made up their minds to get rid of us that way." He slid open the glass door and stepped onto the balcony. The wind gusted angrily, and icy rain hammered down from a slate grey sky like a vertical, turbulent ocean. Kinnaird did not notice that he was drenched within seconds. Below, almost empty, the restaurant carpark stretched out in front of him, a ten-feet drop. Then, surprisingly, he spotted the bulbous shape of a Jaguar Mark Ten just beneath him, its roof barely six feet from the balcony edge. He called to the women, "We'd better go out this way, we can jump on to a car roof."

Mowatt, shivering with cold, dragged Ash to his side. "Hang on to her, I'll fetch some clothes."

"We don't have time for modesty, besides the rain's keeping everyone indoors. Jump down while you still can!"

"But we'll freeze to death!"

"Or fry here. It's your choice." He grabbed the blonde by the arm and pushed her towards a balcony rail. "By the way, Debbie, you don't have one."

"It's a long drop," Mowatt said, staring down.

"Aim for the Jag's roof." He pointed at the car immediately below them. "It'll cushion your fall." She hesitated, listening to the rain spatter against the ground. Below, the Jaguar's roof silently beckoned, the only escape route. Mowatt handed him the gun, climbed over the railing and jumped. Her fall ended with a loud clump that echoed above the rain. A moment later she slid to the ground and waved for the next one. "OK, Debbie, now it's your turn."

The blonde pulled free and backed towards the glass door, her face fearful. "I won't jump!"

"This place is going to blow up at any moment, there's no other way out!"

"I'll take my chances inside." She jumped back into the room and yanked the door closed before he could reach her. An automatic lock secured it. All he could then do was rap his knuckles against the glass and watch her rummage through a pile of clothes. Then she swung back towards him, gun in hand. He jumped over the balcony rail and dropped to the car roof as a shot rang out behind him. He bumped down heavily, wrenching an ankle, and a pain, not unlike the one in his head, tore up his leg as he slipped to the ground. Mowatt was there to support him, shivering, as he placed an arm across her shoulders.

"Did she hit you?"

"No, I just landed badly. We're still too near this place, we'd better get across the carpark." The wind and rain battered them with a million drops of iced water as they staggered towards the exit until he couldn't ignore Mowatt's shivering. He pulled off his soaking shirt and threw it over her shoulders. "We've got to get you inside, this'll make you decent."

"Thanks." She slipped her arms into the sleeves and did up a single button. The distant echo of a gunshot, and zing of a bullet striking close had them diving for cover. They lay flat against the sodden earth, amongst streams of rushing water. Mowatt stared back towards the restaurant. "Was it Debbie?"

"No." His eyes searched the street as the slate grey sky darkened, the heavy rain increasing in strength reducing visibility further. When he finally spotted them, it was almost like seeing an apparition, blurred shapes, a pair of indistinct outlines darting between a row of parked cars close to the restaurant: Duffy and his gunman. They came towards him, their gun flashes brilliant in the grey darkness of rain. "I'll try to pin them down. You crawl away and get help."

"I can't leave you like this!"

The rain almost drowned her voice as it drummed against the ground, an unyielding torrent. Kinnaird stared at her, briefly ignoring the danger. In that moment he spotted things about the way she looked he had previously missed, such as how her dimples seemed more pronounced when she was scared, and her usually smooth brow rippled with creases. "One of us has to get help, and you can move faster than me."

Another bullet zapped the ground in front of them. Kinnaird ducked his head. When he looked up again Mowatt was crawling away on her stomach. He bid her a silent farewell and fired at the hazy outlines in front of him. Both instantly disappeared throwing up a splash of water as they hit the ground. Then Debbie Ash appeared in a doorway, still nude and holding a gun. She spotted Duffy and fired, the gun flashes dazzling even through the downpour. In an instant the restaurant disappeared in a furious belch of flame and thunder that rocked the earth. Kinnaird covered his head with his hands as building parts joined the rain and showered down. In less than a minute he lay surrounded by debris, while a cloud of smoke rose from the roofless ruin that remained. He pushed himself to his feet, tucked the gun under his trouser waistband and limped back towards the restaurant. The Jaguar had been thrown on to its roof, beneath it two pairs of legs stuck out at odd angles. Duffy and the gunman would have died without realising it, while, somewhere close, Debbie Ash joined them. Kinnaird lacked the strength to look further, and moved away as sirens echoed in the distance. When he reached the road people had begun to emerge from nearby buildings, drawn out by the explosion. He drifted through them searching for Mowatt until an arm reached out from a Volkswagen Beetle and caught his hand.

"Del, I'm here." A door opened and he joined his partner in the front of the Volkswagen. She sat behind the wheel, trembling, eyes anxious, his wet shirt barely concealing the shape of her heaving breasts.

"Where'd you get the car?" Something stirred on the seat behind. Too late he realised they still had trouble as keen, icy steel pressed against his jugular.

"Glad you could make it, Kinnaird," Mona Curtis taunted.

"I wondered what had become of you." Slowly, and with

the blade teasing the veins in his neck, he turned to meet her gaze.

"Worried about me, were you?" she gibed. "OK, sister, drive us out of here. Head towards the river, I'm taking you for a swim."

"What's the point, Mona?" The blade cut into his skin and he began to bleed.

I came back for Debbie," Curtis snarled with a flash of perfect white teeth. "I saw you struggling with her on the balcony. Why didn't she jump?"

"She was too scared, she wanted to take her chances by going through the restaurant . . . . I tried to stop her. You must have heard her shoot at me before I jumped."

"I didn't hear nuthin' but the rain, but I saw you struggling with her, that's all I know." Ahead of them a police car, its blue roof light flashing, led a convoy of fire engines into the street. Kinnaird stared at them, "Looks as if the cavalry's arrived."

"Too late for you!" Curtis kept the blade poised against his neck as they passed the emergency vehicles. The smoking ruins of the restaurant ensured that everyone on the street had their attention focused in its direction, and the Volkswagen slipped away unnoticed.

"As I was saying," Kinnaird continued, hoping he could talk Curtis out of murder, "Debbie was scared of jumping, there was nothing I could do."

"You should have tried harder or better still kept out of it. We almost had it all."

"All of what?" Kinnaird repeated, genuinely curious.

"Debbie and I were angling for a takeover of both camps ever since we got close. We were almost there, almost the queens of vice . . . . Then your little friend put in an appearance and Duffy didn't die, she ruined everything!"

Mowatt sighed. "Duffy's men twigged me immediately, but I didn't expect to be taken prisoner. I couldn't do anything, they had a knife and took me upstairs. That's when we walked in on Mona and Debbie fighting with their boss."

"But how could you take control of both rackets?"

"There was no one to stop us. You'd taken care of Fisher, and Hodgkiss was working for us. We had that perv sewn up so tight he couldn't pee without asking our permission. The south was virtually ours. The north as well, since you'd gotten rid of Macaulay. Debbie was trusted in both camps and could have taken over without creating any ripples. With me to support her here, all we had to do was remove Duffy."

Realisation is a strange thing when it comes suddenly because it feels like a slap in the face. Kinnaird saw all the pieces of the jigsaw in the blink of an eye. "You murdered all those people, you and Debbie!"

"Sure we did. We piggy-backed on Hodgkiss, knowing how he got his kicks. Debbie suggested that he come north to beat Duffy's girls, and Fisher jumped at the idea, especially as we'd got his women to complain they couldn't take more beatings. It put Fisher and Duffy at loggerheads while we did the real manoeuvring, everyone was distracted, including you. I slit Tina Wilson's throat just after Hodgkiss beat her up, did it right in front of him. He couldn't believe it. Then I pulled out a shooter and made him handle the blade until his fingerprints were all over it. I dropped the blade into a plastic bag and left him there. He went berserk next time he saw Debbie, but she showed him some photographs of him beating up the other dead girls, including Tina's kid sister."

"I still don't get it," Kinnaird frowned. "Hodgkiss is big

league, he could've gone to the police and told them everything. The worst he could have been charged with was GBH and, since there were no complainants, even that would've been impossible to prove. On top of that I'm sure he's big enough to ride out any adverse publicity. Besides, some people think powerful men have a string of toms on call anyway. There was certainly more chance the police and courts would believe his version of the story than one provided by a couple of toms."

"That's right," she replied coolly. "But Debbie had another ace. She found out that he was working scams at the Stock Exchange with insider information. One afternoon she photocopied some papers while he slept. He's as crooked as the rest of us. From that moment on we had him. He was with me at the hospital, we wanted him present whenever an attack took place."

"You gambled that he wouldn't talk when arrested?"

"We gambled on us wastin' him before you pieced things together and took him in, but you beat us to it. If you hadn't he'd have ended up a corpse like Duffy should have been. After we heard about his arrest we had to move fast, there was a chance you'd initially doubt what he might tell you about us. You had Fisher, a transvestite, and Hodgkiss' bed partner. No one would've doubted that Fisher could slit a whore's throat. They were both pervs, and it would've been easy for people to accept that their bedtime games had progressed into something more sinister. We figured Hodgkiss would get bail, even on a murder charge, his wealth would see to that, and we'd have killed him. No one would've known."

"It's all gone wrong, Mona. Why don't you simply quit while you're ahead and get away? We were only ever pawns in this."

"If Debbie was still alive I might have done that, but she's dead, and you're the reasons why. Both of you!" She grabbed Mowatt by the hair without taking the blade away from Kinnaird's neck. "Head for Putney Bridge, bitch!"

The rain didn't ease as they arrived at the junction with Fulham Palace Road and turned towards the bridge. The wiper blades swung monotonously back and forth, shifting gallons of water in an effort to keep it clear. Around them traffic was light while pedestrians were nowhere to be seen.

"You know what, Mel?" Kinnaird looked towards her, his head buzzing with an idea. "If you really loved me as you say you do, you should've let me go past the car without stopping. That way Mona would only have gotten one of us."

"Is that the way you would have wanted it?" She glanced back at him, uncertain, a question in her eyes.

"I thought there was more to you two than just police work," Curtis scoffed.

"It happens," Kinnaird told her.

"Spare me the shit, Kinnaird. She's a good looker and I bet you couldn't wait to get your hands on her. You're the same as every other bloke I ever met."

"You've been a tom too long, Mona. It's made you a cynic. Maybe it even turned you into a lesbian. You're so used to bonking your brains out for a living, you only see men as a meal ticket, but not every woman's like that, thank God!"

"You might've sweet talked yourself into this girl's panties, Kinnaird, but you and me know that you're no different from any other animal with a dick." She released Mowatt's hair and leaned close to the detective. "I had a real relationship, with someone who saw things the way I did, and it was the most beautiful thing I've ever known. Someone like you could never understand that. We almost made our dreams come true, but you two stopped us!"

"The best laid plans of mice and . . . . " Kinnaird winced as the blade cut into his neck.

"Del, shut up!" Mowatt snapped. "She's going to murder us soon enough without you bringing the time forward by taunting her!"

Ahead, Putney Bridge came into view.

Curtis eased back on the blade. "I don't think she wants to see you die, Kinnaird."

"Of course I don't!" Mowatt exploded, nerves ragged with dread.

"Pull up when we reach the centre of the bridge," Curtis told her calmly, as if they were simply going for a stroll. "Then, sister, I'll cut your throat first so you don't have to see him die."

They were halfway across the bridge when the Volkswagen stopped. Mowatt's hands were trembling, something she couldn't control. She hoped no one noticed and kept them gripped around the wheel.

"Before we die," Kinnaird said. "Would you let us have a last kiss?"

"Sure, if you don't mind my knife resting against your jugular while you do it," Curtis laughed.

Kinnaird drew Mowatt towards him by the shoulders, her eyes full of fear yet still questioning. As her hands came away from the wheel and moved against him, she brushed the butt of the gun tucked in his waistband. Their mouths met and, whilst his eyes remained open, hers closed.

"That's enough!" Curtis snapped. "It's more than Debbie and I got!"

They parted, the gun in her hand, her eyes open. Then

he recognised something in the way she looked at him, and recalled she had told him she couldn't shoot anyone in cold blood. The blade moved gently across his throat, teasing him with death, and all at once he knew that Mona Curtis meant him to be first. He closed his eyes and waited for it to happen.

"Good riddance, Kinnaird!"

In the small confines of the car the crack from the gun was deafening. The main bitch died with a surprised look in her eyes before the knife fell harmlessly away from Kinnaird's throat.

The rain stopped abruptly, leaving the air heavy with moisture. Staring out across the river, both wrapped in a blanket they had taken from the Volkswagen, Mowatt and Kinnaird leaned against a railing. She was distant, thinking about an assortment of plans she had made what seemed a million years ago. "Do you think that I make a good cop, Del?"

"Not bad, but then I'm biased, you just saved my life." He hesitated. "However, I'd be grateful if you'd do it again."

"Save your life, how?"

"Don't tell anyone that we shared a blanket with you in the nude. If Vienna ever got to hear . . . . "

THE END